MCCAFFERTY MECHANICS

A DEEPWOOD MOUNTAIN COMPLETE SERIES

LEXI HAYES

Published by No Regerts Press, LLC

NO REGERTS
PRESS, LLC

Cover Designed by R Agung Nugraha

ISBN 978-1-957933-38-2 (print)

Join my mailing list here:
www.lexihayes.com

CONTENTS

STEEL STROKE

POWER PLAY

FILTHY FIX

ROUGH RIDE

STEEL STROKE

CHAPTER 1
LILY

The neon sign above the Rustic Ridge Bar buzzes like a hornet, casting an angry red glow over Jake's contorted face. The humid summer air clings hot and sticky to my skin, but his grip is ice-cold as his fingers dig into my arm, putting more bruises on top of the ones already there.

"You think you can just walk away from me?" he snarls, whiskey and rage sour on his breath.

I wrench my wrist free, pain shooting up to my shoulder. "I'm done, Jake. *Done*." The words taste like freedom, sweet but terrifying.

He laughs hollowly, a sound that scrapes my nerves raw. "Right. Where you gonna go? I'm doing you a favor keeping you around, bitch. I could have any woman I damn please."

I shake my head. "Then let me go."

"No. *I* decide when I'm done with you." His hand flies out, shoving me backward, hard. I fall to the ground, gravel biting through the tears in my jeans.

No one wants you, he'd hissed last week, fist twisting my hair. *You're garbage.*

A large shadow detaches from the wall of the bar—a man,

tall and broad-shouldered, his boots heavy on the ground. "Problem here?"

Jake whirls, chest puffed out, ready to fight. "Mind your own business, asshole."

The stranger steps into the light, and my breath hitches.

He's older…mid-forties, maybe…with silver streaking his dark hair and stubble shadowing a jaw sharp enough to cut glass. Tattoos slither up his corded forearms, ink swirling over knuckles that flex once, twice. His eyes lock on mine—dangerously dark green, stormy and unreadable—and for a heartbeat, my entire universe tilts. There's a sudden ache low in my belly, and raw hunger unfurls in my chest.

"I think the lady would like you to leave," he says, his deep voice vibrating through my very soul.

Jake scoffs. "Lady? That's a laugh." He turns and lunges for the guy.

The stranger moves faster, ducking the first punch, then catching Jake's fist mid-air on his next swing. There's the sickening crack of cartilage snapping and Jake crumples, clutching his nose, howling. Blood seeps through his fingers.

"You're dead!" Jake spits, scrambling up.

Suddenly headlights slice through the parking lot and a police cruiser rolls to a stop, with one quick siren and flash of colored lights. Relief floods me as an officer steps out.

"Zane." The officer nods at the stranger, then eyes Jake. "What seems to be the trouble here?"

Zane. The name suits him, rough edges and quiet danger.

"This guy grabbed the lady and shoved her to the ground, Deputy Barlow."

"Bullshit! He hit me!" Jake screams, showing the officer his bloody nose.

Zane blinks calmly. "He threatened me—"

"And Jake swung first," I chime in, voice hoarse.

"You lying cow!" Jake thrashes and yells as the deputy cuffs his wrists. "You'll pay for this. You're *mine*, Lily. Don't ever forget that. *Mine!*"

Time to stand up for myself. I give the deputy the information he needs to press charges. Then the officer pushes Jake into the cruiser.

As they drive away, I wipe my palms on my jeans, Jake's screams chasing me, clawing at the fragile calm settling over my bones.

"You okay?"

I jump. Zane stands close, not touching me, but I can feel the heat radiating off him. He smells like motor oil and cedar soap. His gaze sweeps over my body, not leering but definitely assessing, lingering on the bruises on my arm.

"I'm fine," I whisper. My knees tremble, the adrenaline crash near.

He grunts, seemingly unconvinced. "Where you headed?"

Nowhere. The word lodges in my throat. My duffel bag, pitifully light, leans against Jake's pickup. Some clothes, a couple of sketchbooks, and thirty-seven dollars hidden in various places, including my boot, bra, and front jeans pocket.

Jake always wanted to make sure I had nothing, so I would have to rely on him and him alone.

Zane's jaw tightens. "Got people nearby? Family or friends you can call?"

The parking lot blurs. I shake my head miserably, humiliation scalding my cheeks.

The silence stretches out, only the songs of cicadas in the background. Then, gruff and quiet, he says, "I've got a couch."

I blink up at him. His eyes are guarded, but there's no pity there. I watch his throat bob as he swallows.

"Why?" The question pops out before I can reel it in.

He shrugs, flannel pulling across shoulders broad enough to hold up entire worlds. "Don't like bullies, I guess."

A laugh bubbles up within me, sharp and broken. "But I'm a complete stranger."

"I know your name's Lily. You heard the deputy call me Zane. We're not *complete* strangers." He gestures for me to follow. "C'mon. You can crash at my place, then work at my shop tomorrow to earn your keep."

Work. A job. The offer is a lifeline but doubt still coils in my gut. Men don't offer to help for free. Jake was already teaching me that when I was seventeen. *You'll pay your way, princess.* I've learned that lesson in blood, bruises, and more.

And yet…Zane's gaze doesn't slither over my body like I'm used to. His hands stay shoved in his pockets like he's afraid to touch me.

"What kind of shop?" I ask.

"Motorcycles. McCafferty Customs."

"Is that the shop from the reality show?" I watched it for a while because Jake liked it. Then he realized all the guys were drop dead gorgeous and he got jealous. I never got to see another episode.

Zane nods. "Dash McCafferty is my cousin. I co-own the shop with him now."

I smile. "Really? Do you ride?"

He jerks his chin toward a vintage Harley parked near the bar, its chrome gleaming under the streetlight.

Wow. Art on wheels. I've always loved sketching bikes —the curves of the metal, the promise of speed. The sketchbook in my bag's crammed with drawings of them, images pulsing with freedom. My fingers twitch, craving a pencil.

"I don't know what I'd be good at," I admit. "I don't know engines or anything."

"Can you sweep floors, answer phones, and take inventory? Like, count and organize stuff?"

"Sure."

"Then you're hired." He turns toward the Harley, then pauses. "Here. You'll need this."

My duffel dangles from his fist. When did he grab it?

I reach out and take the bag, our fingers brushing. His rough skin rasps over mine, sending a tingle up my arm. His green eyes snap to mine, darkening.

Wow, I could get lost in those eyes.

"Thank you," I whisper.

He nods stiffly once and strides over to the bike. I follow, my heart hammering.

He tosses me his helmet. "Wear this."

I put it on as he swings a leg over the Harley, then I climb up behind him. The engine growls to life, vibrating through the soles of my shoes.

I cling to his waist, hyper aware of the way his bulky muscles flex under his jacket. His back is solid as a mountainside, heat seeping through layers of fabric. We tear up the winding road, the pine trees blurring into black smudges, the night air sharp with the smell of sap and gasoline.

For the first time in years, I feel...awake. *Alive.*

The cabin appears out of the gloom like a mirage—logs weathered to smoke-gray, a porch light haloed in moths, glowing like a beacon.

"Some ground rules," he says, killing the engine. "Anything in the pantry and fridge is fair game. Just leave a little of the good Scotch for me."

He glances back as we head in, an almost-smile playing on his lips at the startled laugh that punches out of me.

Inside, the living room smells like pine resin and leather. Zane tosses me a blanket and pillow from a linen closet. "Bathroom's down the hall. Towels are on the rack next to the show-er." His brow furrows. "Oh, and careful of the coffee maker. It's temperamental sometimes."

I nod and hover by the couch, duffel hugged to my chest. "Why are you doing this?"

He stills. For a heartbeat, pain ghosts across his face. "Saw my old man hit my mom once," he says quietly. "Wish some-one'd stopped him sooner."

The confession hangs between us. I want to reach out. To trace the silver in his hair and ask him to tell me more. But instead I just whisper, "Thank you."

He nods abruptly and vanishes down the hall. A door clicks shut.

The couch sags under me, but it's soft and warm. Through the window, I take in the looming mountains—ancient, indif-ferent. I know somewhere below, Jake's cursing my name. But here, I feel like I can breathe.

For now.

CHAPTER 2
ZANE

The smell of coffee drags me awake.

Not *my* coffee—mine's bitter, strong enough to strip chrome. This smells...sweet. Vanilla? The kind of fancy shit Dash's wife drinks.

I sit up, the old bedframe groaning in protest. Last night replays in jagged flashes—Lily. The bar. Those awful bruises. The way she latched onto my waist as we rode on my bike like I was the last anchor in a stormy sea.

I scrub my hand over my face, stubble rasping against my rough palm. I shouldn't have brought her here. I'm too old for this. Too broken to have this sweet young thing occupying my mind.

But the alternative, leaving her alone in that parking lot, wasn't an option. Not after seeing the fear in her eyes. And yet, she stood her ground. Gotta admire that.

The wood floor creaks down the hall.

I jump up and grab a quick shower, then pull on some jeans and a clean flannel. By the time I hit the kitchen, she's there too, leaning against the counter in those shredded jeans, eating

9

yogurt. Her hands are remarkably steady after what she's been through.

Her chestnut hair is damp and dark around her pale skin. She looks even younger and softer in the morning light...and absolutely beautiful.

Sun filters through the window, catching a fresh bruise on her neck, purple and angry. Almost like a brand.

My fists clench. *Fucking asshole.* Should've punched the bastard harder.

"Mornin'," I grunt, reaching past her for the coffee pot. A sudden, possessive surge rushes through me when I notice that her hair smells like my shampoo.

"I figured out the coffee maker," she says softly. "I don't know how you take it, but I can add milk and vanilla, like I did to mine—"

"No need," I say hastily. "Black is just fine."

I pour a mug, then hesitantly take a sip. It's strong. Full-bodied and rich. "Very good," I say, then nod to her sneakers and the soles peeling off them. "Shop's no place for those. We'll stop by Harriet's Tack and Feed and get you some things before work."

She flinches. "I can't afford—"

"It can come outta your first paycheck," I lie. Harriet actually still owes me for the carburetor I rebuilt for her nephew's bike last month.

Her shoulders relax. "Okay, thanks."

The ride to town is even more tortuous than last night. No darkness to hide in now. Just her thighs pressed to mine, her warmth seeping into every part of me she touches. Every damn bump and pothole makes her grip my body tighter. By the time we pull into Harriet's, I'm hard as a piston.

Harriet's Tack and Feed is a relic—peeling paint, a rusted bell over the door that jangles like an old crow's caw—but it's well stocked. I ask Harriet to find Lily some sturdy boots and other appropriate work clothes and put it on my tab. Then I wait outside, trying to get my head on straight.

She comes out later in steel-toed boots, some carpenter-style Dickies, a proper T-shirt, and a flannel shirt. She's got a bag with some extras as well.

Christ, she's a knock-out. I'm doomed.

The shop's already buzzing when we arrive. Kyle's laugh echoes over the growl of a '78 Shovelhead. Dax is cursing at a stripped bolt from under a lift as Remi hip-checks a tool chest across the grease-slicked floor.

"Move your ass, Shaw!" Remi hollers, brandishing a socket wrench at Kyle as if to lob it at him. He ducks, throwing her a grin.

Lily freezes next to me, wide-eyed.

"Welcome to the circus," I mutter, steering her inside.

Heads turn and the Shovelhead engine sputters dead.

"Holy shit," Kyle drawls, wiping grease on a rag he then stuffs into his back pants pocket. "Boss brought a girl." He ambles over, tugging at his Judas Priest tee.

"You're late, Boss," Remi says, eyeing Lily as we walk up. "You the new meat?"

I'd tell Remi to back off, but her smile is teasing rather than predatory.

Lily shifts, fussing with her sleeves. "Guess so."

"This is Remi," I say. "Anything breaks, she can fix it. She can also be meaner than a rattlesnake, but she don't bite."

"Hmph. Not what I heard," Kyle murmurs out of the corner of his mouth, waggling his eyebrows.

Remi flips him off.

Dax emerges from under the lift, flexing his arms. "Hope you like tetanus, sweetheart."

Lily's chin lifts. "Hey, I've had my booster shots."

Dax chuckles.

I glare at them all. "This is Lily. She'll be answering the phones, cleaning, running errands, that sort of thing. Don't be dicks."

"Anything you need," Lily adds. "I'm a fast learner."

Kyle snorts. "Anything?" He looks her up and down. "You're too pretty to be doing grunt work. We should get her on our ads, Zane. Maybe in a skimpy bikini and—"

"Keep going with that," I growl, "and you'll be scrubbing oil pans with a toothbrush."

Kyle grumbles and half salutes. "Got it." He smiles at Lily. "I'm Kyle—I know everything there is to know about vintage bikes, but not so much about when to shut up, sometimes."

"Tell me about it," Dax groans.

"Dax here is a whiz with steel and tech," I say. Then I gesture to the office. "Why don't you start on the supply closet? It needs organizing. Any way you think it would work best. We're not particular."

I get her settled and leave her to it.

Dax crosses his arms and huffs when I return. "Hate to say it, Boss, but with those soft hands and scared eyes, she won't last a week."

Something hot coils in my gut. "She's tougher than she looks."

By eleven, the supply closet's gone from a warzone to neat as a pin.

Lily's covered in dust, a few strands of hair escaping her

12

ponytail, and clutching a clipboard as she's organizing a crate of spark plugs.

I swear I could eat her up whole.

Amazingly, she's somehow tamed the chaos. Brake pads line the shelves like library books. Nuts and bolts gleam in mason jars labeled in loopy script.

I lean against the doorframe, blinking. "The torque wrenches look so...organized," I say, awestruck.

She jumps. "Oh! I didn't hear you." Then she laughs nervously. "Um...yes...I arranged them by size and torque rating," she says. "I hope that's okay?"

"Better than okay." I reach over and brush my thumb over a label she made where she drew a tiny motorcycle. "And these sketches are incredible."

She shrugs, but I notice her cheeks are tinged pink. "Pfft, they're just...doodles."

"They're *good*." I look down at her, and she glances up at me. The air is suddenly charged with electricity. A wicked image of her on her knees before me bursts into my mind.

Get it together, McCafferty.

She clears her throat. "Everything else is sorted by type, size, or whatever seemed most relevant. If there's anything you want me to change, please let me know." She points to a clipboard hanging on the inside of the door. "I made a chart showing where things are kept, too," she announces, almost triumphant.

I flip through it. She's made more little drawings of the items for clarity. "This is great."

She smiles. "And I, um, found these." She holds up a box of vintage spark plugs—rare as hens' teeth. Been missing since Dash's bachelor party. (Don't ask.)

I chuckle. "Kyle might propose marriage if you show him these. He's been looking for them everywhere."

She giggles sweetly.

"Holy shit!" Remi exclaims, scanning the closet as she walks up. "Boss, we're keeping her, right?"

I fight the smile that's threatening to take over my entire face. I feel like a giddy teenager. "Of course we are," I laugh. Lily's already getting led away by Remi, who's promising to give her the full tour.

Through the window of the office, I watch her. She's nervous at first, jumping when the air compressor hisses or one of the lifts drops. But soon, she's scanning part numbers and drawing up orders, hair twisted up into a messy knot, tongue darting out to wet her bottom lip.

I'm obsessed.

McCafferty, you're screwed.

CHAPTER 3
LILY

McCafferty Customs hums with testosterone and machinery—the growl of a lathe biting into steel, the roar of a welding torch, Kyle's off-key rendition of *Ring of Fire* echoing from the bathroom. And there's a weird smell in the air... like grease and gasoline.

It's totally different from the so-called "reality" show.

Ironic, huh?

For starters, Remi, Dax, and Kyle weren't on it. Just Dash and a crew of larger-than-life mechanics. Probably actors, or at least mechanics with ambitions of acting, or getting shops of their own. I've heard producers manipulate those shows to ensure drama and romance and all that stuff that makes people tune in episode after episode.

Honestly, I like the shop better how it is now. Vintage bike posters on the walls, tools everywhere—it's much more laid back. Grittier for sure, but real. And kinda...exciting.

I follow Remi as she strides past a disassembled Harley, her neon-green streaked hair catching the fluorescent lights. She's tall, lean, and very goth. A total badass, too.

"So, the main office on the left is Zane's lair. He spends a bunch of time there, but he prefers to be out here with us. Because we're all hella cool to be around...and, duh, he likes getting his hands dirty." She winks at me and I try not to blush.

"This is the break room." We walk into a small alcove of the garage where there's a fridge, a sink, and a picnic table. "We try not to have it looking like a biohazard zone. But men... fuck, they can be pigs." She glowers in disgust.

"Bathrooms are down the left side. Fortunately, you and I have our own." She pumps a fist in the air. "The rest of the place, except for that storage closet that you took from *ABANDON HOPE ALL YE WHO ENTER HERE* to *PLEASE COME IN AND BEHOLD WITH WONDERMENT* is for working on bikes in various stages of build or repair."

Dax's massive, booted feet stick out from beneath a lifted motorcycle. How does he get his hulking body under there? "Careful, new girl," he grunts. "Floor's more slippery than Kyle's pickup lines."

"Hey now!" Kyle pops up from behind an engine block, grease smeared across his cheekbones like war paint. "My lines are vintage charm." He waggles his sandy blond eyebrows at me. "Ever ridden a Dyna Glide, darlin'?? She's got curves that'll make you—"

Remi chucks a rubber hose at his head. "*Dude.* Give her at least a couple days before you bombard her with that shit."

Kyle pouts. "But she's gonna be taken by then! All the hot ladies get snapped up!"

"Please, *I'm* single," Remi says.

"I rest my case."

Remi lunges toward him, and he ducks behind the bike as I laugh. "I'm *kidding*! You're hot! You're hot!"

Then I hear Zane's voice rumble from the office, low and

gravelly as he argues with a supplier. "—told you last time, we don't buy cheap gaskets." My heart skips.

Remi follows my gaze. "Don't worry, he's all bark," she says. But *I* know he's got bite, too, from what I saw last night. When it matters.

"Crusty exterior, marshmallow core," she continues. "Don't tell him I said that, though." She smiles and leads me past workbenches coated with decades of grime, and a wall decorated with vintage license plates.

She tosses a wrench in a toolbox with a loud clatter. "You'll get used to the noise," she says, wiping grease off her hands with a rag. "Most of the time these idiots communicate in grunts and tool sounds."

Kyle pokes his head around the corner, grinning. "Don't listen to her. We're a refined bunch. Last week, Dax actually said 'please' when he asked for a hex key."

Dax's snort echoes from beneath the bike. "Bullshit."

I'm only half listening to their banter. My gaze keeps drifting back to Zane. I catch glimpses of him through the doorway to his office—leaning back in his chair, feet propped up on the desk, fingers drumming on his thigh absently. His sleeves are rolled up, his tattoos flexing as he gestures. I wonder if the ink has any particular significance. Wonder if he'd ever let me sketch it.

"Eyes over here, newbie," Remi teases, snapping me back. Heat floods my cheeks. She smirks. "Don't worry about it. He's been staring too."

Before I can stammer a denial, Kyle lobs a crumpled soda can at her. "Wouldja stop traumatizing the rookie? You'll scare her off before lunch."

By noon, my nerves have settled down into something like belonging. The shop's apparent chaos in fact has a rhythm that I'm slowly learning.

"Pizza!" a male voice booms, and I see Dash McCafferty coming through the garage with a stack of boxes. "Eat up before Dax inhales it all," he says, heading for the break room.

I almost drop the phone as I finish talking to a customer. Dash is tall, broad-shouldered, with a handsome face and piercing blue eyes. He looks older than I remember from the show, with more gray in his hair, but it's been a few years now. Honestly, he's more impressive in person.

I can definitely see a family resemblance as Zane walks up to him. "What are you doing here, cuz?"

"Thought I'd drop by, see how things are going," he says, his voice warm. His eyes land on me, and he smiles. "Heard we have a new recruit."

Zane gestures to me. "Yeah, this is Lily. She's going to be helping out around the shop."

"Dash McCafferty." He extends a hand, his dimples flashing. His grip is firm. "Nice to meet you, Lily. Welcome to the family."

Family. The word sends a strange shiver down my spine. It's a dangerous concept, and one I've never gotten too attached to in the past. But looking around the garage, at the new and mostly smiling faces (not sure yet if Dax actually smiles) and the easy camaraderie, I can't help but want to be a part of it.

"Th-thank you," I manage, feeling overwhelmed...and, okay, maybe a little starstruck.

"She's seen the show," Zane explains.

Dash grins. "Man, that feels like ages ago. So much has changed."

"Yeah, you've got a wife and kid now," Kyle says, whistling. "Who'd a thunk?"

"Shut it, Shaw," Dash says, rolling his eyes. "Speaking of which," he says, pulling out his phone, "I gotta pick Brynn up from school. We're going to visit Mommy—I mean, *Willa*—at the library today."

Kyle howls as Dash scrubs a hand over his face. "Fuck, I'm never going to hear the end of that now."

Even Zane is smiling as Remi and Dax break into laughter.

"Bye, Lily," Dash says, leaning close to me. "Enjoy the pizza, you ungrateful little shits," he calls out to the rest of them as he heads out the door.

Once the laughter has subsided, we cluster around the table in the break room, the scent of warm pepperoni and cheese cutting through the oil.

"So, Lily. Where'd Zane dig you up?" Remi asks, grabbing a big slice.

The question hangs in the air as I pick at my cheese. "Parking lot of the Rustic Ridge."

Kyle chokes on his Coke. "Seriously? What, did you owe him money?"

"Kyle…" Zane warns with an exasperated sigh.

"No," I say quietly. "I was…trying to leave a bad situation with a boyfriend—well, ex-boyfriend now. Zane stepped in."

Dax stills, a slice of pizza halfway to his mouth. His fingers tense around the crust.

Kyle's expression turns serious. "Got it. Well, you're in the right place. We don't stand for that shit here. We eat guys like that for breakfast." He mimes cracking bones.

Remi shrugs. "I mean, he's not wrong." She hesitates. "Your parents around these parts?"

I swallow and look at Zane. "No parents. I grew up in foster care."

"Damn," Kyle mutters.

Dax chews louder, frowning.

Remi takes another bite. "Siblings?"

"Nope. Just me," I shrug, feigning nonchalance.

19

Zane shifts in his seat, and I feel his gaze on me...warm and persistent.

"Well, you've got us now," Remi says with a smile, tossing her crust into the box.

And as I look at them around the table, I think she's right.

CHAPTER 4
ZANE

I'm trying to be professional here.

I really am.

But *damn*, Lily is undoing me with every shy smile and sideways glance.

My heart pounds like it wants to break free from my chest. I haven't been drawn to someone like this in years, probably not since my ex-wife. The marriage ultimately crashed and burned, making me bury feelings and desires like these deep down so they couldn't hurt me again. But this girl makes me feel like a teenager again.

It's been less than a day, and I can't stop thinking about her. I'm not sure what the hell to do about it.

I watch her from the doorway of the office, her slender form bent over a box of parts, clipboard in hand. She's taken to this job like a duck to water, organizing and cataloging with an efficiency that's both impressive and frankly slightly terrifying.

The supply closet's now a fucking work of art—filled with her detailed, whimsical drawings that are all her.

She catches me staring, and a small smile tugs at her lips before she looks away, a soft blush staining her cheeks.

Damn it.

I'm too old to be getting hung up on a girl barely out of her teens. To be feeling this pull, this fierce need to protect, to claim, to possess.

But there's something about her, something in those wide, expressive eyes, in the set of her shoulders, in the way she moves through the world like she's ready to take flight at any moment. She's a paradox: fragile yet strong, timid but bold, broken and still whole...

And I'm drawn to her like a moth to the proverbial fucking flame.

Later in the day, I notice a couple of Summit Auto Parts delivery guys loitering outside by their truck, eyes fixed on Lily crossing the garage. Their eyes rake over her, lingering where they shouldn't.

The office window's open. "Hot damn, McCafferty. Hiring eye candy now?"

Sudden fury surges through me. I drop my feet hard onto the concrete floor and stalk out to them. The guys straighten up, trying to look busy.

"Watch it, boys," I growl, as my fingers curl into fists.

The taller one—Dave, I think—flinches. They exchange a glance, their smirks fading. "E-easy, man," Dave stutters. "Just admiring the new hire."

I take a step closer, my eyes locked on theirs. "She's here to work, not be your fucking entertainment. You so much as look at her the wrong way again, and I'll let your boss Burt know you're dicking around on the job. Understood?"

They nod, eyes wide, and scramble to leave. I watch them go, swallowing my anger as best I can.

When I turn back, Lily's standing there, looking at her feet.

"I... I didn't mean to cause any trouble," she says in a small voice.

I sigh, running a hand through my hair. "You didn't, Lily. They're just a couple of idiotic kids."

She nods, but I can tell from the way her shoulders hunch and her amber eyes flick away that she's embarrassed. Self-conscious. And it kills me.

Before I can stop myself, I reach out and take her elbow. "Come here," I say, my voice rough. I lead her into the office, closing the door quietly behind us.

"Hey." I take a step closer, my hand reaching out to smooth a strand of hair out of her face. "Don't let pricks like that get to you, okay?"

She shrugs, throat bobbing. "It's okay... I'm used to it."

The resignation in her voice snaps something loose in me. My hand strokes over her jaw, thumb brushing the swell of her lip. It's so damn soft. Her tiny exhale at my touch threatens to undo me.

"You *shouldn't* be okay with it," I grind out. "I don't know you that well, but seems to me you've been through hell, and you're still standing. Still fighting. That's something to be damn proud of and makes you one of the strongest people I know. And assholes that treat you as any less deserve to be told to fuck right off."

Her lashes lower, and heat licks up my spine as she leans into my touch. She clutches at my shirt, her lips part, and I can see the pulse fluttering in her throat. My heart races, my body suddenly alive with a hunger that's almost painful.

Fuck.

I dip my head, close enough to taste her breath...sweet, like the cola she had at lunch—

The office phone rings.

We jerk apart, and Lily's chest heaves as she backs away.

I grab the receiver. "McCafferty Customs," I bark into it, glaring at the wall.

It's Dash. Of. Fucking. *Course.*

∿

The rest of the day, I make a point to avoid Lily no matter how much I want to be near her.

It's too risky—and at work, too! I'm her goddamn *boss*, for god's sake. What is wrong with me?

The cabin is quiet when we get home, the silence a complete one-eighty from the chaos of the shop. Lily disappears into the bathroom, the click of the lock final. I lean against the kitchen counter, my head bowed, my body still throbbing with unfulfilled desire.

I can still feel her baby soft skin under my rough hands. Still see the way her eyes turned dusky at my touch.

It's killing me. It's fucking *killing* me.

I push away from the counter, my boots heavy on the hardwood as I stalk into the living room. I need a distraction, something to take my mind off her, off this hunger that's eating me alive.

Lily's bag is on the couch, her sketchbook peeking out from the top. Its edges are worn and frayed, as if it's been stuffed into numerous duffels, tucked into a multitude of pockets. I hesitate, my hand hovering over it. I shouldn't look. I know I shouldn't. But I can't help myself. I pull it out and flip it open.

I nearly choke.

The pages are filled with drawings—landscapes and portraits, abstract designs and intricate patterns, all rendered in exquisite detail. There are a few sketches of the shop, of the bikes...of the guys. There's even one of me, bent over an engine, my brow furrowed in deep concentration. When did she even have time to do them?

They're good.

Really good.

But it's the self-portraits, raw and honest and full of emotion, that really get to me. I can see her in every line, in every shadow and curve. I can see her strength, her vulnerability. Her fears.

It's absolutely breathtaking.

Footsteps pad down the hall. I look up and she freezes, wearing an extra large T-shirt I gave her to sleep in, her hair still damp from a shower. When she sees me with her sketchbook, her face pales.

"That's...private," she whispers.

"I'm sorry, I should've asked first." I open the sketchbook to a page with a magnificent drawing of a Harley. "But Lily... Why hide these? You're incredibly talented."

"I..." She stammers, taking a step back. "They're nothing."

"Nothing?" I huff out a laugh. "You're brilliant, Lily. An artist! You should be doing this for a living."

She takes the sketchbook from me, her fingers brushing against mine. I almost groan at the electric zing.

Her eyes meet mine. "You don't have to say that," she says, sitting down next to me on the couch.

"Why not? It's the truth. You have a gift. A real, honest-to-god gift. And you need to believe in it. Believe in yourself."

Her eyes shimmer, and she looks away, her fingers tracing the edge of the sketchbook. "I-I just... I never thought I was good enough, or that anyone would care about what someone like me could create."

I slide my fingers under her chin and tilt her face up. "You are more than good enough. You deserve to have your art seen. You deserve to make your mark in this world, just like everyone else."

A tear slips down her cheek, and I brush it away with my

thumb. Her eyes are full of hope and fear and longing, and it's scrambling both my mind and body.

"Don't ever let anyone...especially shitheads like Jake... make you feel small," I add.

She bites her lower lip, and I can't resist her this time.

Just as I'm about to lean in, she surges forward herself, lips crashing to mine, desperate and hungry. A groan tears from my chest as she fists my shirt, pulling me closer. Every swipe of her tongue feels like a challenge.

And fuck, I want more.

I push her back against the armrest of the couch, her hips meeting mine, grinding against my hard, aching cock.

Christ. She's on fire, teeth nipping my lip, nails pricking my scalp.

"Zane—" she whines. I swallow the rest of it. She arches into me, her soft curves against my hard angles, her nipples two sharp points. Every gasp, every shiver's music to my fucking ears.

Her heartbeat thunders against mine very fast.

I worry that *this* is too fast.

I rip myself away, panting. "We can't."

Her cheeks are flushed as her chest heaves. "Why not?"

Because you're too young. Because I'm your boss. Because it's barely been two days...and because I shouldn't hold you back from your life.

I lean back, running a hand shakily through my hair. "You deserve better than an old motorcycle mechanic who couldn't even make his first marriage work. You don't need my baggage."

Her brow furrows. "You're going to talk to *me* about baggage? Please. At least have the decency to tell me the truth —that you don't want to get involved with someone who has enough baggage to drown in."

I grab her wrist. "That's not—"

"Let go of me, Zane," she says, getting up from the couch.

"But Lily—"

She shoots daggers at where my hand is holding her wrist, so I release it.

"Thank you," she says, her tone telling me she's done with this conversation.

I get up. "Night," I say. Then I head to my room, our words hanging between us, raw and tight.

Maybe she'll decide that I'm not worth the trouble.

But…damn, that doesn't sit well with me, either.

CHAPTER 5
LILY

The dull ache in my chest is a constant reminder of last night.

Zane's rejection stings, but I understand it. I'm a mess. He's got his own issues—I can't blame him for not wanting to take on mine as well.

But understanding it doesn't make it hurt any less.

I'm just a pit stop. A charity case. A kid.

We dance around each other all day, polite and distant. Every time he brushes past me, I tense up, my body remembering the heat of his hands, the scrape of his beard on my skin, and the sound he made when I sucked on his lip.

I crave him, but can't have him. It's torture, pure and simple.

Remi notices, of course. She's perceptive as hell, and she doesn't miss the way I flinch when Zane's voice rumbles too close, or how his eyes track me when he thinks I'm not looking.

"You two are beyond exhausting," she sighs, twirling an oil catch pan on her finger. "Look, just either fuck or fight. This tension is killing me."

I choke back a sputtering laugh. "Jesus, Remi!"

She grins, unapologetic. "Hey, I call it like I see it. And what I see are two people who want each other but are too scared to do anything about it."

I shake my head, but her words strike a chord. I do want him. More than anything. But I can't force him to want me back.

"Hey." Remi slings an arm around my shoulders. "We're hitting the Ridge tonight. You in?"

"In?"

"Pool. Pitchers. Bad decisions." She grins, smearing grease on her coveralls. "I'm not taking no for an answer. We'll let off some steam, have some fun. Initiate you in the McCafferty Customs Crew. It's mandatory...and, well, you need this."

She has a point. I *do* need this. A chance to unwind with my new friends sounds nice.

~

The Rustic Ridge is packed, and filled with laughter. Country music blares from the sound system, and the clack of pool balls cuts through the bar noise. We manage to commandeer a corner table just as another group vacates it, and Kyle immediately orders a round of beers.

Zane sits across from me, his eyes hooded and unreadable. He's wearing a black Henley that stretches across his chest, the sleeves pushed up to reveal his tattoos. Ugh... My heart pounds just looking at him.

He's ridiculously, painfully sexy.

I tear my gaze away, trying to focus on the conversation around me. Remi's telling a story about a biker rally she went to last summer, gesticulating wildly. Kyle's laughing, his eyes crinkling at the corners, and even Dax—yes, *Dax!* —is chuckling.

I force myself to laugh and join in, but my awareness of Zane is off the charts and I can't ignore him, no matter how hard I try. Every shift of his body or rumbling laugh sends an unholy shiver through me.

Remi challenges me to a game of pool, dragging me up with her. "Come on, Lily." She glances over at Kyle. "Let's show him how it's done. He can play the winner."

I'm a terrible player, but I take a cue anyway, chalking the tip. Zane's eyes follow me, and I *might* put a little extra sway in my hips as I lean over the table.

Remi breaks, scattering the balls with a sharp, decisive crack. She sinks two solids right off the bat, and Kyle groans. "Damn it, woman. Leave some for the newbie."

She smirks. "Don't tell me what to do with balls, Kyle."

I'm up next. I lean over the table, lining up my shot. I can legit *feel* Zane's gaze on me, hot and heavy, and my heartbeat speeds up. I take a deep breath, trying to steady my nerves, and strike the cue ball.

It spins wildly, missing my target completely, and I groan, standing up.

"You're distracted," Remi purrs, sinking her next three balls with a smirk. "And really shit at pool."

I huff. "I know."

Kyle leans against the wall, grinning. "No kidding. She's got it *bad* for Daddy McCafferty."

I choke on my beer. "*Daddy?!*"

"Look at him." Kyle gestures with his bottle. "All scowly and protective. If that's not daddy energy—" He pales. "Shit. He's looking over here. I think he knows what I'm saying."

Zane peers in our direction. He *does* look like he can understand Kyle.

"When the hell did he learn to read lips?" Kyle says worriedly. Remi chuckles and heads to the bar just as Zane's gaze turns directly on me, molten and hungry. I press my thighs together, the memory of his hands on me last night flaring bright.

God, I want him.

Remi reappears next to me with a tequila shot. "Liquid courage, girl."

I knock it back, fire searing my throat, and grab my cue. I'm about to shoot when I look up and see someone pushing angrily through the crowd.

Jake.

He's flanked by two guys I don't recognize, his nose taped up and his lip curled in a sneer. The room tilts when his eyes lock on me, venomous. "Hey, girl."

Zane's already moving toward me, a predator on the attack. However, Dax beats him to it—all 6'7" of his hulking muscle blocking Jake's path.

"You lost, little boys?" Dax looks down at them, cracking his knuckles.

Jake tries to stand taller. "Out of my way, Lurch. I'm here for what's mine." The other guys snicker.

Zane is beside me in a second, his hand on the small of my back, glaring at Jake. "She's not a goddamn possession."

Jake laughs, cold and sharp. "Oh, snap. What, you her daddy now, old man?"

The crew closes ranks: Remi with a pool cue, Kyle cracking his neck, and Dax standing as still as a marble statue with a bad attitude.

"She doesn't need a daddy. She needs someone who respects and supports her. Treats her like the amazing woman she is. And that sure as hell ain't you," Zane scoffs.

Jake inhales sharply, eyes darting between us and the

group, calculating. "This isn't over. She's *my* bitch!" He spits at Zane's boots, but Zane doesn't flinch.

"Walk away, Jake," Zane seethes. "Now. Before I break even more of your pathetic face."

Jake's eyes go wide and the crew presses in tighter when he makes like he's going to charge them. But then Jake's guys start backing up, and eventually he follows suit. "Come on guys, this bar's full of skanks and overgrown roaches."

They turn to go, shoving people and chairs angrily as they leave.

When they're gone, I let out a breath. Zane's thumb strokes my spine, rough and grounding. "You okay?"

No. I'm shaking. Furious. Ashamed. How could I ever have thought that man was worth my time?

"I'm sorry," I whisper.

His jaw tightens. "Don't you dare apologize."

"I'm just so stupid."

"Hey! No," he says, grasping my face. "You are *not* allowed to say that. He's the asshole here. And tomorrow morning I'm taking you to Sheriff Quinn's office and we're going to get you a restraining order for that dipshit. Okay?"

I nod, trying to shake off the guilt.

"Come on, I'm taking you back to the cabin."

The crew all gives me hugs or fist bumps as we leave, then Zane and I are back on his bike, my arms around his waist, the vibration of the Harley between my thighs a cruel mimicry of what I crave.

When we arrive, Zane parks too fast and kicks out the stand like he's angry at the ground.

He's upset. But I know he's not mad at me, and that just makes me want him even more. I trust him more than I've trusted any other man I've ever known.

Inside, we drop our things and just stare at one another for a moment, there in the dark, just a sliver of moonlight coming through the window and catching the sides of our faces.

"Lily—" he finally begins.

I quickly press my palms to his chest, feeling his heartbeat thudding.

"Don't say it."

He stills.

"I'm twenty, not twelve, you know. I know what I want."

"You deserve—"

"I want *you*," I blurt, cutting him off. "All your broken pieces and baggage. I'm *not* your ex-wife, Zane."

Something snaps in him.

He pins me against the door, his mouth capturing mine, hot and desperate. I moan, arching into him as his hands rip at my clothes.

"Fuck, Lily," he groans, his lips trailing down my neck as he strips off my clothes. "I need you. Need to taste you."

Once he has me naked, he lifts me up and I wrap my legs around his waist. He carries me quickly to his bedroom and lays me gently on the edge of the mattress, his eyes blazing like wildfire.

He gets down on his knees and tears off his shirt. My god, his chest is a masterpiece—all those thick muscles and striking tattoos. "Spread your legs, baby," he grits out, and I get dizzy.

My legs fall open at his command.

The look in his eyes is downright feral as he lowers his head. His breath is hot on my skin when he presses a kiss to my pussy. I moan, my hips instinctively rolling toward him. He chuckles, the sound vibrating against me.

"Patience, sweetheart," he murmurs, looking up at me with a wicked grin.

He teases my wet folds with his mouth, then circles my clit

with his tongue. I gasp as pleasure zings and zips through me, making my legs tremble.

I dig my fingers into his scalp as he licks and sucks on my most sensitive flesh, his tongue tracing intricate patterns until I'm writhing and begging on his bed.

"Zane," I gasp, my body tightening, the pleasure building. "Please. I'm so close."

He looks up at me, his eyes dark and intense. "Let go, Lily. I fucking need to taste your sweet honey."

His tongue becomes even more ruthless—circling, sucking, licking, creating stripes of fire that leave me breathless. I fist the sheets, his name a broken chant as he drags me higher and higher.

"Ohh-*hh*!" I finally cry out, coming undone with a scream, my body convulsing. He licks me through it, slowly and deliberately. I'm left a pile of boneless, quivering limbs.

When I open my eyes, he's looming over me, pupils dilated, lips glistening. "You ready for more, baby?"

I surge up, kissing him deep, tasting myself on his tongue. "God, yes," I murmur.

CHAPTER 6
ZANE

I growl, my body aching to possess her. To claim her.

I roll her onto her back and move away to pull off my jeans and boxers. My cock springs free and she gasps.

"Damn, Zane," she whispers, and I grin, searching my nightstand for a condom. There should be one way in the back, I think? I finally grab hold of one, and with relief tear it open and roll it on.

"There we go…" I say, crawling back over her body, hips settling between her thighs. She wraps her legs around my waist, her heels digging into my back, urging me on.

Reaching between us, my fingers find her slick and more than ready. I groan, my cock throbbing with the need to be inside her. I position myself at her entrance, my eyes locked on hers, and slowly, carefully, I push inside.

Her breath catches and her nails dig into my shoulders as her body tenses beneath me. I go still, giving her time to adjust, my body shaking with the effort it takes to hold back.

"You okay?" I ask, voice rough.

She nods. "Yes. *God*, yes. Please… Keep going."

She doesn't need to ask twice. I begin to move, my hips

rocking slowly, carefully, each stroke drawing a gasp from deep within her. She meets me thrust for thrust, her back arched, her breath coming in short, sharp pants.

I can feel her pussy tightening around me, her body clenching, her release getting nearer. *Fuck me...*

She moans, her head thrashing from side to side, her body writhing beneath mine.

"That's it, baby," I murmur, my voice thick with desire. "Take me. Take all of it."

My own release builds, my body coiling like a spring. I'm close, so close.

"Zane," she gasps, her eyes locked on mine. "Come with me."

Her climax hits her hard and that's all I need. I roar, my body shuddering along with her, my release crashing over me. I pour myself into her, my body convulsing and my breath ragged.

We're both shaking, holding each another tightly until at last I collapse on top of her.

Spent. But my heart is full.

She falls asleep first, her breath warm against my collarbone.

I slip out of bed, pulling on shorts and padding to the living room. The moon paints the cabin in silver, and the creek out back beyond the porch murmurs like it's keeping secrets.

My mind is a whirlwind of thoughts, each one fighting for dominance. I'm thinking about Lily, about the way she felt beneath me, the way she moved with me, the sounds she made when I touched her.

I'm also thinking about the bruises on her skin, the fear in her eyes when that bastard Jake showed up at the bar. And I'm thinking about how much I want to protect her, to keep her safe, to make her happy.

It's that last one that really scares me.

I've been here before. I've felt this pull, felt this need to protect and provide. I've let myself fall, let myself believe that I could be enough for someone. And I've been burned. Badly. My ex-wife made sure of that. She took everything I had to give and then some, leaving me with nothing but a heart full of scars.

What if that happens again?

What if I let myself fall, only to crash and burn? Lily deserves better than that. She deserves someone whole, someone who can give her the world, not just shattered pieces of it.

But the thought of letting her go, of watching her walk away, is like a knife to the gut. I can't bear the idea of her not being here, not being mine. It's only been two days, but she's already become a part of me, a part of my world.

And I don't want to let that go.

I need advice. Need someone to tell me what to do, how to navigate this tangled mess of feelings.

Dash.

He's the closest thing I have to a brother, the one person I trust to tell me the truth, no matter how much it hurts.

It's late but I text him anyway, my fingers shaking slightly.

Me: *I'm in deep, man. I can't stop thinking about her, but I'm also so fucking scared. What the hell do I do?*

I hit send and wait. The minutes tick by like hours, each one stretching my nerves taut. Finally, my phone buzzes with a response.

Dash: *You stop sabotaging your shot at happiness, that's what you do. You've been given a second chance here. Don't fuck it up by letting fear control you. You deserve this, Zane. Stop being a pussy and tell the girl what you want! And then go back to sleep!*

He finishes with a kissy face and moon emoji.

I read the words over and over. It finally sinks in, and I laugh. Dash is right.

I'm an idiot.

I slide back into bed and pull Lily close to me. She nuzzles into my chest, breath warm on my skin, body fitting perfectly against mine.

"Stay with me, Lily," I murmur, my voice soft, my heart pounding. "Stay here and be mine." I pause. "Not like a possession. But mine to love and cherish. Completely."

She blinks and looks up at me, her eyes shining. "There's no place I'd rather be," she whispers, her voice thick with emotion. "I'd love to be yours, Zane."

We seal the deal with a kiss.

A long, deep one.

The next morning when I head out into the kitchen, I find her sketchbook open on the coffee table to a new drawing—my cabin, the mountains, two motorcycles side by side. Scrawled in the corner: *Home.*

She appears and hands me a mug of coffee. "Got up mega early and couldn't help myself. What do you think?"

"I love it," I reply. "And I love you."

Her smile is as radiant as the sunrise. "I love you, too."

EPILOGUE - LILY

SIX MONTHS LATER

My fingertips trace over the glossy curve of a fuel tank I spent hours hand-painting this week—flames licking over the midnight chrome, rose gold flecks catching the garage lights above. Every brushstroke on these bikes is a labor of love, proof that I really am an artist, like Zane said.

He was right: I just needed to believe in myself.

It feels like just yesterday that I didn't know how to hold a wrench or add up an invoice. Now, the shop purrs under my management. Orders for client commissions fill the whiteboard in my precise block letters, and my framed design sketches hang beside Zane's vintage motorcycle blueprints. McCafferty Customs isn't just his sanctuary anymore. It's ours.

The crew says I have the gift of a "steel stroke"—the magic I wield with my paintbrush on the bikes. And yes, I know there's a double-entendre in there somewhere, since Kyle can't help but snicker every time he mentions it.

I kick off my boots, the concrete floor now shiny and clean ever since I've been running things. It's cool through my socks as I head toward the office. The shop's been closed for a few hours and it's quiet, the daytime chaos replaced by the faint creak of the roof settling. I stayed late to finish a concept for a client in Denver, a lady wanting her late husband's Harley rebuilt into something "worthy of Valhalla", as she put it. Zane offered to wait up, but I hadn't expected him to actually stay.

Yet there he is.

Slouched asleep in the battered recliner he won't let me throw out, head tipped back, arms loose at his sides. The soft glow of my desk lamp paints him in golden light, silver dotting his stubble and throughout his thick hair, the collar of his Henley stretched wide to reveal the dragon tattoo I traced with my tongue last night. His chest rises and falls slowly and steadily, a half-empty coffee mug set dangerously close to the edge of the desk.

My heart does that thing it's done since the very first time I saw him—stutter, swell, and pound with excitement.

I crouch beside the chair, drinking him in. The scar on his eyebrow from an exploded tire. The calluses on his palms. The way his lashes flutter, restless even in sleep. Two years ago, I wouldn't have dared speak to someone like him, let alone touch him. Now, I know every dip, ridge, and contour of his body better than my own.

I nudge the mug to a safer spot on the desk. He shifts, but doesn't wake up.

"Zane," I whisper, brushing my lips over the pulse at his neck. It jumps under my mouth.

He mumbles something gruff and unintelligible, hands flexing like he's reaching for me.

I smile against his skin and slide down to unbuckle his belt.

He stirs when I unzip his fly and tug his jeans down his hips a little. "Lily...?" he mutters, his voice gravel-deep with sleep.

"Shh." I press a finger to his lips. "Let me take care of you."

His eyes flicker slightly open, but he doesn't move. Just

watches me through heavy lids as I free his cock, already thickening in my palm. His length and heft still impress me every time.

I lick slowly from base to tip, savoring the salt-sharp taste of him, the velvety weight on my tongue.

"*Fuck, baby,*" he rasps, hips twitching.

I take him deeper, one hand stroking his balls. His rough groan vibrates through me as his fingers scrape the chair arms. I love this—the power that I feel from reducing him to guttural sounds and trembling muscle. He tangles his hands in my hair, not pushing, just *holding*, like I'm something sacred to be cherished and revered.

"Look at me," he grits out.

I glance up, our gazes locking.

I suck harder, swirling my tongue, and his head falls back with a ragged curse. "Jesus, Lil. Gonna make me come so hard if you keep doing that."

His words only spur me on, swallowing him deep again, humming around him. His hips buck, his cock hitting the back of my throat. Tears prick the back of my eyes, but I don't stop. I want this, want him unraveling, want to feel his release spurting hot down my throat.

"*Lily—*" His warning growl is my favorite sound.

I slide a hand under his shirt, nails raking his abs, and he snaps. With a roar, he spills into my mouth, fingers now fisting my hair. I swallow every drop, milking him until he's shuddering, until his grip gentles to trembling caresses.

He hauls me into his lap, crushing my mouth to his, tasting himself on my tongue. "You're gonna kill me," he mutters against my lips.

I straddle him, grinding down on the hardness still there. "Please. You loved every minute of it."

"Damn right I did." He nips my jaw, hands sliding under my shirt. "Take all this off."

I oblige, stripping slowly, his gaze scorching every inch of skin I reveal. When I'm finally out of my jeans and panties, I climb back onto his lap and sink onto his cock that's already rock-hard again.

He grips my hips. "Christ, you feel good."

We move together, roughly, desperately, the chair squeaking beneath us. His mouth finds my breast, his teeth grazing my nipple, and in moments I'm coming with a wild cry, clenching around him. He follows seconds later, burying his groan in my neck.

We stay like that, tangled and breathless, until the sweat dries on our skin.

"Marry me," he murmurs, nuzzling my hair.

I jerk my head up, blinking repeatedly at him. "What?"

He leans back, his dark green eyes serious. "Marry me. Properly. Church, dress, the whole shitshow. I want the world to know you're mine."

Tears blur my vision. "Zane..."

He swallows, uncharacteristically nervous. It's adorable. "I want *everything* with you, Lily. Kids. A family. You pregnant with my baby, all round and gorgeous, cursing me for knocking you up while I rub your swollen feet."

A laugh bubbles out of me. "You've thought about this a lot."

"Every damn day." He plays with a strand of my hair. "Whaddya say, beautiful?"

I kiss him, staking a claim on his lips. "Yes."

He grins, boyish and bright, and stands with my legs still wrapped around him. "Good. Now let's go home. Gotta start working on that first baby."

I laugh as we quickly put on our clothes. He carries me to

the door, our shadows merging on the shop floor. Outside, the mountains cradle a sky smeared with stars.

I'm beyond happy. My art's both hanging on the walls and sought after by clients for their bikes. The man I love wants to start a family with me.

I used to think freedom came from running. Turns out, it's from putting down roots.

Zane sets me on the Harley, his arms winding around me as he revs the engine. "Hold on tight, soon-to-be Mrs. McCafferty."

The name fits like destiny.

And as we roar into the night, I know I'll never let go.

POWER PLAY

CHAPTER 1
KENDRA

The bumpy road to McCafferty Customs jostles my latte in the cup holder, and I curse as it spills down the side of my car's otherwise pristine center console.

Great. Now it'll be sticky until I have time to get it detailed. And who knows when *that* might be.

I should've grabbed some wet wipes at...what was it called? Nolan's General Store? Yeah, that was it...as I drove through Main Street. Assuming a store in a town this small actually *has* such things.

Remind me again why I am taking on a client in Deepwood Mountain?

My brother Mitch's name flashes on my dashboard screen for the umpteenth time today. He'd already been pressuring me to move to Deepwood to be closer to him and his new wife Penny ever since we reconnected. I wasn't sure, but when he mentioned in passing that a local motorcycle mechanic needed representation for a bogus lawsuit, I saw an opportunity to prove I'm more than just a corporate shark. I really do want to help people. *All people*—even people in tiny towns that may or may not have wet wipes.

47

I touch the screen and Mitch's text pops up.

> Dax doesn't talk much, but he's a good guy.
> Just don't let his size scare you.

I dismiss it with a quick swipe, scoffing. I don't scare easily, even if my brother's idea of "good guys" included his parole officer at one point.

I can certainly handle an overgrown motorcycle mechanic.

After another fifteen minutes, my destination comes into view, a brick garage surrounded by mountains of steel salvage and motorcycle parts. I park in a small area off to the side and get out of my car, immediately accosted by the industrial smell of fiberglass, gasoline, and solvent. The place is loud, too, with growling engines and buzzing power tools. There's a startling clang followed by someone yelling, "Kyle, you idiot, that's my fucking *foot*—"

I adjust my tailored pencil skirt and crisp ivory blouse, wondering if I really needed to opt for this kind of attire here.

Strangely, I'm hit with a sudden flutter of nerves. I face down judges and opposing counsel without batting an eye, but there's something about this place that has me on edge. Maybe it's the thought of stepping into such a different world. Or maybe it's because I'm completely on my own now, without the support of a big, prestigious firm behind me.

But hey, it was my decision to go solo with my law practice.

I take a deep breath and look up after retrieving my bag from the passenger seat.

And that's when I see...*him*.

A man behind the garage, bare-chested, wielding a hose like he's auditioning for next year's edition of the *"Hot Mechanics & Their Filthy Bikes"* calendar.

Sunlight glints off the water arcing over a chrome motorcycle. It reflects off the sweat slicking his absurdly defined back muscles, too. His tattoos ripple as he scrubs the bike's fender, jeans sitting low on his hips.

Wow, this must be Dax.

Mitch wasn't kidding. The man is a *wall*. A six-foot-seven brick house. One that I could lick from top to—

He turns and sees me just as a gust of wind hits. The hose shifts and water sprays out into the blustery gale.

All over me.

"Son of a—" I shriek as icy water soaks me. My silk top clings to me instantly, the lace bra underneath now on full display to all of rural Montana.

Dax whips around, the hose still spraying. His eyes—my god, they're the color of cognac—widen momentarily. "Shit!" He fumbles with the nozzle, accidentally dousing his boots. *"Fucking hell..."*

He lunges for the spigot and finally kills the water.

Too late. I'm already a dripping wet mess.

Dax grabs a towel and strides over, still shirtless and smelling like motor oil, sweat, and pheromones that tease my core.

Here." He thrusts the towel at me. "It's all I got."

I take it and wrap it around myself as he stares, scowling and scratching his scruffy jaw.

"Sorry, ma'am." Grr. I hate *ma'am*. What am I, fifty?

Snickers come from the garage and I whirl around, rolling my eyes, indignation primed. A woman all in black with neon green streaks in her hair gives me a sympathetic thumbs-up and then punches the other guy in the arm for laughing.

"Back to work, you two," Dax growls, and they move deeper into the garage.

"Dax Thomas?" I ask, checking my hair tentatively, thankful it's stayed put in its tight bun.

He nods. "That's me."

"Kendra Brooks. Dash asked me to come down."

"Right. You're the lawyer. Mitch's sister," he replies.

I tap my wet briefcase and sigh. "If they're not all soaked, I'll give you a card." I glare at him. "Do you have a minute to talk now?"

"Sure," he says, gesturing for me to follow. "Let's go to the office."

"One request, Mr. Thomas." He looks back at me and I gesture to his bare torso. "Can you please put on a shirt?"

His lips twitch ever so slightly as he opens the office door, pulls a faded T-shirt from a hook on the wall and puts it on, the fabric straining across his massive shoulders and chest.

Suddenly I'm not sure if I'll be able to focus on anything this man says.

CHAPTER 2
DAX

S he stands in my office like a glacier in July—somehow still polished and shimmering even as the water clings to her dark hair.

I didn't mean to drench her, but turning to see her walking toward me like some corporate fantasy woman come to life had me frozen. With her hair pinned up tight, that skirt fitting her curves perfectly and her high heels showing off those gorgeous legs, I thought I was dreaming.

Not holding a hose into the wind.

And then seeing that cream-colored lace bra peek through from under her soaked top before I gave her that towel...

Brutal.

She looks too young to be a lawyer: the confidence in the set of her shoulders usually only comes with age. She's scanning her surroundings like a hawk, sharp sapphire eyes darting over the filing cabinets, the stack of unopened parts invoices from April, the coffee mug I welded together last year. Her nose twitches, probably unused to the lingering scent of coolant and metal.

I lean against the doorframe, blocking out the noise of the

shop. "Have a seat." I nod at the chair across from Zane's desk. If only he was here to deal with this crap. But he and Lily deserve a honeymoon far away from work.

She pulls the chair out. "Thank you, Mr. Thomas." Her voice is pure city—sleek vowels, clipped consonants. She sits, her spine ramrod-straight, one hand holding the towel closed at her chest, the other resting primly in her lap.

I sit on the edge of the desk in front of her. I can't help but notice how her gaze snaps to my arms when I roll up my sleeves.

Heat drags up the back of my neck. "It's Dax," I say. "Mr. Thomas is—"

"Your father?" she interrupts.

I shake my head. "No. He's *Dr.* Thomas."

"Oh." She licks her full, dusky lips, and all my blood rushes to my groin.

"I was going to say, 'Mr. Thomas' is for those I haven't doused with my hose."

She huffs out a small laugh. "Funny." She unlatches her shiny leather briefcase. Thankfully, it didn't get too wet. "Now, tell me about the lawsuit."

"Some rich kid claims the brake lines on his custom Kawasaki burned out mid-ride." My thumbnail picks at dried flecks of sealant on the desk. "Says it's my shoddy work that made him crash."

She pulls out a tablet, begins scrolling. "He's lying."

I freeze. "How would you know?"

"I've seen your shop." She nods toward the bay doors, where Kyle is screwing in a bolt under a bike on a lift, laughing at something Remi's shouting. "And I'm aware of your reputation. Mitch says no one here half-asses anything."

My chest does something stupid and warm. It's nice to know people see the hard work I put in and have my back.

She slides the tablet toward me and points to zoomed-in photos of a mangled motorcycle, the brake lines severed. "These weren't frayed from wear. They were deliberately cut."

I pick up the tablet and swipe. A close-up of the line's cross-section shows the edges crisp, with no corrosion. My pulse kicks into high gear. "This isn't my work."

"Of course not." She tilts her head, the overhead lights glinting off the gold chain at her throat. "And look at the lower fluid reservoir. See those weld marks?"

I do. They're jagged, amateur. My hand curls into a fist. "Some idiot modded it post-delivery."

"Exactly." She leans forward, and *Christ*, that blouse is still see-through, every button a dare. "Is there anyone you can think of who would want to frame you?"

Viper. The name curdles in my gut. He's probably pissed that I told his now ex-wife he was cheating on her last year. But this damned siren's blouse has me struggling to form words, so I just grunt. "Competition's cutthroat."

She studies me carefully. "You're not telling me everything."

"And you're wet."

The words just pop out and her cheeks flush pink. Fuck, that shouldn't be so sexy.

"Yes, because *someone*," she says icily, "doesn't know how to handle his hose."

A laugh punches out of me, rough and dirty. "From the looks of you, I think I handled my hose just fine."

Her eyes go wide and she clutches the towel more tightly.

The air thickens, the office suddenly as hot as a kiln.

After a pause, she clears her throat. "We need proof the bike was tampered with *after* it left your shop. Any receipts? Witnesses?"

"The jerk was a tourist. Just passing through, you know?

Bike left here six months ago." I rub my beard, thinking. "Viper's crew deals in chop jobs. He could've intercepted it."

She looks up from the tablet. "Viper?"

"Rival builder. Also a total snake. He runs a shop near Bozeman."

She taps a manicured nail on the desk. I suddenly imagine those nails clawing down my back in the heat of passion.

Focus, dammit.

"We'll subpoena his records," she states. "Track the timeline."

I snort. "He's not going to keep receipts for sabotage."

Her blue eyes flash. "Then I'll talk to his employees. Someone'll crack."

"Or you'll get your pretty throat cut." The warning comes out growlier than I intended. But the thought of her getting hurt—or worse—makes me angry.

"I doubt you've ever set foot in a chop shop." I stand, looming over her. "They'll eat you alive."

She leans back to look up at me and the towel falls off her shoulders. "I've cross-examined CEOs who make mobsters look tame. I'm sure I'll be just fine."

Our eyes clash, mine coffee-bitter, hers ice-sharp. She smells like rain and something flowery, or maybe citrusy. I shouldn't be this close to her, not now that I can see the outline of her stiff nipples in that bra. I could so easily toss her onto the desk, climb over her and—

"Dax! You wanna come check this torque?" Kyle calls from the garage.

I step back. "In a minute!" I yell. "This isn't your world, Kendra," I continue, rubbing my neck.

She pulls the towel back in place, covering herself up and folding her arms. "Well, we need evidence."

"The Grizzly Summit Rally is this weekend. I'm sure Viper and his crew will be there. Kyle and I can—"

"No, I'll go! Viper and his guys don't know me. I'll get them to talk."

I stare. "You? At the Grizzly Summit Rally?" The poor woman's lost it.

"Why not?"

I shake my head. "It's forty-eight hours of beer and loud motorcycles. You'll stick out like a diamond in a scrap heap."

She smiles. "Then show me how to blend in."

The challenge hangs between us. I imagine her in leather, hair wild, laughing into my ear on the back of my bike—

Nope. I slam that door shut. I'm paying her to win a case, nothing more. I'm not getting involved with a damn lawyer, even if she's distracting as hell with legs that won't quit.

But... She's right. No one's going to tell me or Kyle anything. They know us. They know *everyone* from McCafferty Customs.

She's our only shot.

I groan and take a deep breath. "Fine," I finally say. "But you'll be under my watch the entire time. For your own safety."

She nods. "Got it."

"We'll need to make you over, too."

"Really?" She furrows her brow. "I have jeans, boots, and a tight top."

I laugh. "That's not gonna cut it. Come back tomorrow at noon. I'll have Remi fix you up."

"Is that the woman with green hair?"

"Yep. She'll take you from corporate siren to biker babe in less than an hour. Guaranteed."

For the first time today, she hesitates.

"Hey, you asked me to show you how to blend in," I shrug.

She chews her lip, then nods decisively. "What the hell. Okay." She starts packing up her things and hands me a card. It's only a little damp. "Here's my number."

I take it from her, a lick of fire scorching my skin when my fingers brush hers.

She clears her throat. "I'll return the towel tomorrow," she announces, walking toward the office door. She pauses when she gets there. "We're going to win this, Dax."

I huff. Go figure, I like hearing her say my name. "If you say so."

"I do," she says. Then she turns and leaves.

Kyle materializes before me, grinning like a hyena. "City girl's got you twisted, huh?"

I hurl a dirty rag at him. "Shut it."

But I watch her through the window anyway. She pauses at her car—a silver Audi that probably costs more than my custom bike—and glances back.

Fuck, she's caught me staring.

There's a flicker of a smile on her lips.

I'm in big trouble.

CHAPTER 3
KENDRA

I walk into McCafferty Customs just before noon, my mind spinning.

Dax is bent over a bike in the garage, his back to me, tattoos peeking out from beneath rolled-up shirt sleeves, his firm, delectable ass up in the air. My pulse skips.

It was hard enough staying composed yesterday, between my soaked clothes and his gorgeous eyes studying me. But seeing him fully in his element today and that body...ridiculously sexy.

Remi walks up beside me. "Hi, I'm Remi." She offers her hand, her short nails painted black.

I shake it. "Kendra. Nice to meet you."

She grins and rubs her hands together. "Ready to create this villain origin story?"

I blink. "Excuse me?"

She loops her arm in mine. "You know, turning a big city lawyer into a small-town biker chick. That's some serious chaos. Let's go."

What have I gotten myself into?

I follow her as Dax straightens, turning and wiping his

hands on a rag. His eyes rake over me, lingering a beat too long. I...don't mind. "Afternoon, Kendra."

"Dax," I nod.

Kyle emerges from the break room, a massive burrito in hand. "I'm Kyle and this is my lunch." It sounds like something a little kid would announce.

I chuckle. "Hi Kyle, I'm Kendra. You have a Mexican restaurant in town?" I ask. Maybe there is hope for Deepwood Mountain after all.

"I wish," Kyle snorts. "This is from the frozen foods section at Nolan's."

Damn.

Remi drags me to a makeshift dressing area in the break room near a beaten-up picnic table. She holds up a pair of shiny leggings so tight they could easily double as sausage casings. "Leather pants or chaps would've been my first choice, but those need time to break in for the best fit." She nods back to the leggings. "Still, these'll make any man's tongue flop out of his mouth."

"I'd like to be able to walk."

"These are latex. They stretch." She peers around me. "And you've definitely got the ass for them."

I blink.

Five minutes later, the latex grips me like a second skin, paired with a midriff-baring halter top that shoves my breasts way up and chunky black boots that add two inches to my height.

Remi lines my eyes with dark eyeliner, smudges shadow across my lids, then applies a thick layer of mascara. She tugs my bun loose, fluffing and teasing my hair as it tumbles down in waves. Then she runs blood-red lipstick over my lips and has me blot it on a tissue.

"Damn," she murmurs, stepping back. "You're a *problem*."

I turn to the mirror and freeze.

"This isn't exactly subtle."

"Trust me, this is understated chic at a rally," Remi says, adjusting my top. "You're selling 'I can handle a bike and a beer,' not 'I'm here for a bar fight'."

She leans close to whisper in my ear. "But you might just start one, that's for sure."

Dax's voice rumbles nearby. "How's it going in there?"

Remi pulls me from the curtained area into the open. "Tada!"

Dax drops his wrench.

It clatters on the concrete, the sound echoing as his gaze drags up my body. His throat bobs.

Kyle whistles. "Woah… Dax, can you maybe put your tongue back in your mouth?"

"Shut up," Dax growls, stooping to grab the wrench. His ears are tomato red.

Remi smirks in my direction, brows raising. "Told ya."

I fight back a smile.

"Needs something else, though…" Remi says, tapping her cheek thoughtfully. She looks over and plucks a silver chain from a nearby bin and loops it around my hips, just at the bare skin above my waistband. "There," she says triumphantly. "You're officially a biker's wet dream."

Dax steps closer suddenly, his heat searing my side. "That chain's not sitting quite right." His callused fingers graze my skin, adjusting my makeshift belt. I inhale sharply when his thumb brushes the dip of my waist.

My lungs stall. The shop fades away. There's only his scent…oil, cedar, and his own special musk…and the rough pad of his thumb on my skin, like he's committing the feel of it to memory.

Kyle fake-coughs. "Jeez, guys, get a room."

Dax snatches his hand back like I've burned him. "Chain's better now," he mutters, crossing his arms angrily.

Remi is grinning. "Oh, he's *fu*—"

"*Stop*," he roars, and the look he gives Remi is clear.

He nods his chin at me. "She needs a crash course in the lingo, rally attitude, bike culture...the whole nine yards. Get on it."

For the next hour, they coach me on everything from how to walk (bit of a swagger) to how to talk (bit of an edge). They teach me the difference between a chopper and a cruiser, how to tell if a bike's been customized or just modified, and what to do if someone challenges me.

"Always stand your ground," Remi says seriously. "They'll respect you for it."

"And remember, no matter what happens, I've got your back," Dax adds, his voice rough. "Any Kyle will be *my* backup."

I feel warmth spread through me. I know he means it. He'll protect me, no question. The knowledge gives me the last bit of confidence I need.

"All right," Remi says, breaking the moment. "Time to get this show on the road. You've got a rally to infiltrate."

The ride to the rally is pure, sweet torture.

Dax's motorcycle vibrates between my thighs, his back a solid wall of heat as we speed down the highway. My arms are locked around his waist, every shift of his body rippling through me. I'm hyper-aware of his every breath, every flex of muscle.

Kyle went on ahead to get rooms and do some recon, leaving Dax and I on our own. When we stop for gas, he looks at me as I climb off the bike like he's stuck in some internal battle. The black motorcycle jacket Remi has loaned me falls open and his gaze lingers on the boots, my midsection, and finally my chest.

"You look…" He hesitates, voice gravelly.

"Like a biker's wet dream?" I tease. "That's how Remi put it."

"Definitely." His eyes darken.

My core melts. Before I can formulate a response, he kicks out the bike stand. "Want something?"

Is he talking about food, or…?

He nods toward a roadside diner. "Cherry pie's pretty good here."

Oh. "Yes, sounds good."

Geez, get it together, Kendra.

Inside, he orders us two slices of pie and two coffees. I stir cream into mine, then watch him over the rim. His hands are massive around the tiny mug.

"Why motorcycles?" I blurt suddenly.

He downs a sip of coffee. "Besides the beauty, the engineering, and the freedom they represent? They're honest. You treat 'em right, they treat you right in return. No lies. No bullshit."

"Unlike people."

His gaze flicks to mine. "Well…yeah."

The waitress slides our plates onto the table, and Dax nudges the larger slice toward me.

We briefly discuss the plan: I'm to talk to the vendors, ask about custom work, and see if anyone mentions Viper's shop.

"What's the story behind Viper, anyway?" I ask.

Dax's jaw clenches. "Guy's trash. He'd sabotage his own grandma if it meant getting ahead."

"Charming," I mutter.

"And I told his wife…ex-wife, now…about his extracurricular activities last rally season. She's a friend. I didn't like him running around on her."

"Sounds like we have a motive," I say, making a mental note. Then I focus on my pie. He was right, it's excellent.

"You're quiet," he says after a while.

"Just thinking." I trace the rim of my plate, now almost empty. "This is the first case I've taken since leaving the firm. It's liberating. But I'm not going to lie, it's a little nerve-wracking, too."

He frowns, puzzled. "But you were all confidence yesterday."

"I still am. But a little bit of fear is good for motivation."

"Well, I don't doubt you." He leans back, those big, beefy arms crossed.

"Is that a compliment?"

"Observation." His boot brushes mine under the table. "But yeah. It's also a compliment."

The air crackles, and my belly does a little flip-flop.

Dax clears his throat, tossing cash on the table. "Let's go."

CHAPTER 4
DAX

As we roll in, the Grizzly Summit Rally hits me like a flash of adrenaline, a raw, sensory assault. It's an onslaught of chrome: bikes everywhere—custom choppers, pristine vintage bikes, and revving hogs. The air's thick with the sweet scent of exhaust and sizzling meat. Music blasts, engines roar, and the buzz of hundreds of people fills the grounds.

Kendra's grip tightens around my waist as I slow the bike, her body pressed to mine. I've been semi-hard since we left Deepwood Mountain, and that's not helping.

We move past the chaos and reach the motel on the outskirts of the event fields. We didn't want to stay in any of the designated rally accommodations in case people saw us together, so we had to settle for this uninspiring roach palace.

Kyle's leaning against his bike in the gravel lot, smirking like he's won the lottery. "Bad news," he says, jerking a thumb toward the motel office. "Only one room left. Guess you guys'll have to share."

I kill the engine and Kendra slides off the bike like she's done it a hundred times. Smooth as hell.

63

"You're kidding," she says flatly, after pulling off her helmet and shaking out her hair. The latex leggings Remi poured her into catch the sunlight, and I nearly bite through my tongue.

"What about you?" I say, leveling my gaze at Kyle.

"I've got a friend that'll let me stay with her." He smiles and tosses me the key. "Room 12. Only one bed, but hey—" He waggles his eyebrows. "Plenty of floor space for your delicate back, old man."

"I'll snap your femur," I mutter, snatching the key from him.

Kendra's already striding toward the room, her bag in tow. "We'll figure it out. Let's drop off our stuff and get to work."

The room's a disaster—cracked AC unit, sagging bed, and a bathroom smaller than my toolbox. Her perfume cuts through the mildew smell as she tosses her bag on the mattress. "Relax, it'll be fine. We're adults." She glances at the bed, lips twisting in a smirk. "As long as you have something I can sleep in. I didn't bring any pajamas."

I choke on air. "You're joking."

"Hey, I didn't think I'd be sharing a room," she smirks, brushing past me toward the door. Her hip grazes mine, and my whole body twitches. "Let's go before you have an aneurysm."

The rally's already in full swing, a riot of leather, tattoos, and a haze of barbecue smoke. Vendors hawk their wares, bikers show off their rides, and couples dance to the music of gritty guitars.

"Showtime," Kendra murmurs. Then she confidently marches into the fray, melting into the crowd as if she's done it a thousand times. Heads turn as she passes and guys check her out, their eyes lingering on her curves. I almost lose it when she flips her hair at some bearded guy watching her by the beer tent.

"Easy, Hulk," Kyle whispers, elbowing me as I crack my knuckles. "She's *supposed* to flirt."

My jaw clenches tight. "He's got his hand on her back."

"And you've got your head up your ass. *Chill.*"

Kendra laughs at something Beardo says, and the sound slices right through me.

Next she drifts to a vendor booth, leaning over to check out a display of custom pipes. The guy's stare drops to her ass, and I'm halfway to the booth before Kyle yanks me back by my jacket collar.

"You blow our cover and this whole thing's shot," he hisses. "*Trust her.*"

I grit my teeth. "He's wearing a wedding ring."

"So, you can break his nose *later.*"

Kendra writes something on a clipboard the vendor offers her. Probably the fake name we came up with at the diner— *Cherry Douglas.*

I have to admit, she's a natural: flashing a killer smile, laughing like she means it, and striking up conversations as if she's genuinely interested.

Dumbstruck, we continue to watch her work her magic as she saunters toward where we've pointed out Viper's crew near the stunt ring. Her hips sway, chain glittering, and Viper himself straightens up like a bloodhound catching a scent.

"Bingo," Kyle whispers.

My stomach twists.

The guy's all sleaze…a greasy weasel with a rat-tail and serial killer eyes. He slithers up to her in his snakeskin vest, licking his lips like he's already chosen her as his next victim.

Kendra tips her chin up, bold as hell, and my heart jackhammers.

Kyle and I move closer to listen in.

"You're new," Viper purrs, fingers brushing her arm.

"Just passing through town." Her voice drips honey. "Heard this is where the *real* talent hangs out."

Viper's chest puffs out. "Let me buy you a drink, sugar. Show you around."

Every muscle in my body locks up. "That's it. I'm ending him."

Kyle slings an arm over my shoulder, steering me toward the beer tent. "No, you're not. You're getting a drink. She's got this."

"He's got *both hands* on her."

"Yes. And you've got a death grip on my elbow."

I hadn't even realized. I drop Kyle's arm.

Kendra follows Viper to the bar, laughing at his dumb jokes. I'm three seconds from snapping. Kyle shoves a beer in my hand. "Chug. Now."

I drain it in three gulps. "She's touching his arm."

"Brilliant detective work, Sherlock. Let's toast your inevitable heart attack."

Kendra glances over Viper's shoulder, catches my eye, and winks.

The knot in my chest unravels just enough to breathe.

She's got this.

Doesn't mean I don't want to drag her out of here and check every inch of her for bruises.

Viper leads her toward the bike show and I shadow them, Kyle on my heels. She asks questions about custom mods, steering the conversation toward brake lines. Viper's bragging, boasting about his shop's "superior craftsmanship" (fucking *please*), and my fingers are itching to weld his goddamn mouth shut.

"You'd look mighty fine on my newest build," he says, sliding his hand down to her lower back.

I lurch forward, but Kyle tackles me behind a food truck. "*Dax.*"

"He's nearly palming her ass—"

Kendra sidesteps smoothly, and Viper's hand falls away. "Show me the bike," she says, all business. "I want to see if it's as pretty as you say."

Kyle releases me, grinning. "Man, she's playing him like a fucking fiddle."

"I hate this," I spit.

I punch the temporary padding on the light pole next to me. Guess the venue decided to protect their equipment after so many…incidents.

When did I become so possessive?

The moment I saw Kendra, that's when.

As the sun begins to set, the music gets louder, the drinks flow more freely, and the atmosphere becomes charged with a wilder energy. Kendra is in the thick of it, dancing and laughing, her eyes shining with excitement and maybe a *little* too much whiskey.

We stick close to her, always within reach, watching. We're not the only ones: Viper's eyes rarely leave her, and I can see the hunger in his gaze.

Finally, near the end of the night, Kendra makes her way back to us. She's breathless, her cheeks flushed. She leans in close, her breath warm on my ear. "I think I've got him. Viper wants to meet up tomorrow night at his motel room. He said he'd have suggested tonight, but he has important plans he can't break."

"Some douchebaggery, probably," Kyle says darkly.

"His room?" I don't like the idea of her going somewhere I can't watch over her.

She nods. "He's got some paperwork with him. Probably didn't want to leave it at his shop. I'll need to get him to tell me what he did and snap some photos."

"No," I say firmly.

She rolls her eyes. "You have a better plan?"

"Much better. *I'll* go."

"He knows your face, genius," Kyle says, flinching when I lunge his way.

Kendra steps between us and puts a hand on my chest. "He's right. Viper sees you, he'll clam up."

"It's not worth risking your safety."

She smiles. "That's sweet, but you hired me to win this case. I want to clear your name and get this joke of a lawsuit dismissed. You really want your reputation tarnished in addition to paying that dirtbag?"

"Well...no," I finally admit grudgingly.

"Then I'm your only shot, Dax."

Her nail scrapes my nipple through my shirt, and I stifle a groan. "Fine. But I'm going to be right outside that piece of shit's motel room, just waiting for him to fuck up."

Kyle fake-swoons against my bike. "And they say romance is dead."

Back at our room, the air is thick and humid, and the stench of old cigarettes clings to the walls like a grimy film.

Kendra strips off her jacket, revealing that cursed halter top. "I'm showering first," she announces, sauntering into the bathroom.

The door clicks shut.

I stare at the bed.

They called it a queen. Bullshit. It's the size of a postage stamp.

Kyle's laugh echoes in my brain. *Plenty of floor space.*

Yeah, I'm too old to be sleeping on the floor. Especially *this* floor. Can we say *crime scene?*

The shower kicks on.

Hell.

CHAPTER 5
KENDRA

The shower's scalding water does nothing to wash away the memory of Dax's gaze burning into me all day. I press my forehead to the mildewed tile, replaying the way his jaw twitched every time a man got too close to me, or his possessive growls when Viper's hand drifted too low on my back. How his eyes darkened when I caught his gaze, like he wanted to devour me one bite at a time.

Get a grip, Kendra. He's your client.

Steam clings to my skin as I step out of the shower, the motel's threadbare towel barely covering me. The T-shirt Dax loaned me—*"For modesty,"* he'd grunted through the bathroom door before stomping out to find pizza— hangs from the door-knob. The fabric swallows me whole, smelling like him, musky and male, and it's all I can do not to press it to my face and inhale like a creep.

The room feels smaller when he returns. He kicks the door closed with his boot, the casually dominant gesture making my pulse spike. He doesn't look at me, just sets the pizza on the wobbly table and cracks open a beer from the six-pack. "Hope you like pepperoni," he says tightly.

"Classic." I grab a slice and sink onto the bed, one leg tucked under me. "No pineapple?"

"That's an arrestable crime in Montana, counsellor." The corners of his mouth quirk up and my stomach flips. He drags a chair over, the wood groaning under his weight.

We eat in silence. The crunch of the pizza crust and rattle of the rickety AC are the only sounds. I notice every shift of his body, every flick of his gaze toward my bare thighs.

He wipes his mouth with the back of his hand. "Why did you get into law?"

I twirl a string of cheese around my finger. "Honestly? The money. We didn't have a lot of that when I was growing up. I guess I thought making money while fighting for justice would be an honorable profession." I shake my head. "But soon I realized I screwed up. I should've been fighting for the underdog from the beginning. My brother... He could have used that at one point."

His expression softens. "Life's about learning lessons."

"Of course, but... I regret not being there for Mitch when he needed me." The admission stings. "Anyway, I'll always be there for him now."

His beer bottle clinks against the table as he sets it down. "You care, Kendra." He smiles. "That's dangerous in a world that doesn't."

"This from the man who told Viper's wife he was cheating."

His laugh is low and rough. "Snitches get stitches, right?"

"And respect from those that admire men brave enough to stand up to injustice. Like me."

There's a beat, then he stands abruptly. "Gonna shower."

≈

The bathroom door creaks open, steam billowing out. My throat goes dry when Dax emerges wearing nothing but a towel slung low on his hips, water glistening in the valleys of ink and muscle of his chest and abs.

He rummages in his bag, his back flexing, grabs some clothes, and heads back into the bathroom.

He reappears a moment later in basketball shorts, the sharp V of his hips disappearing beneath the fabric. I have to press my knees together to stop the flood in my panties.

"You're wound tighter than a carburetor spring." He grabs a beer, takes a long pull.

"Am not."

He snorts. The mattress dips as he sits beside me, heat radiating through the thin space between us. His voice drops. "My dad's a PT. He taught me some things. May I?"

Say no. Push him away. Be smart, girl.

Instead I turn, presenting my back to him.

His hands slide under my shirt—*his shirt*—callused but gentle as they touch my skin. I nearly go up in flames right there.

"Christ, Kendra," he mutters. "You always feel like you're made of barbed wire?"

He begins kneading out the knots in my shoulders. I bite my lip to stifle a moan. "Comes with the job," I manage to reply.

"What else comes with it?" His fingers slide higher, his thumbs circling the base of my neck.

I stiffen. "Whatever it takes to win. Within reason, of course."

His grip tightens—not painfully, but possessively. "I didn't like seeing those guys leering at you, touching you."

"Jealous?" I mean it as a taunt. But it comes out breathless.

His mouth brushes the shell of my ear. "Incredibly so."

The admission cracks me open, and I involuntarily arch into his hands. He groans, low and ragged, his palms sliding down to my waist.

"Touch me, Dax," I whisper.

Shit, what am I doing?

"Where?" he replies, his breath hitching.

I guide his hand around to my stomach. "Here."

His fingers brush against my skin and I shiver, a gasp escaping my lips. He caresses me, my muscles fluttering under his soft touch.

"Higher," I breathe.

His hands slip around my ribs, just skirting the underside of my breasts. My head falls back against his chest.

"Here?" he asks, setting delightful sparks alight as he draws gentle patterns with his rough fingertips.

"Y-yes," I stutter.

He leans in, his lips brushing against my neck, my breath catching as his teeth graze my skin. "More," I manage to whisper.

His hands cup my breast gently, teasing me, his thumbs brushing against my nipples, eliciting another gasp.

His lips move up to my ear, his breath hot against my skin. "What about here?" he asks, circling my nipples, then working the peaks until they're painfully stiff and aching.

I moan, arching into his touch. "*God*, yes."

One of his hands slides down, slipping inside the waistband of my panties.

"And here?" he asks.

"Yes," I reply, spreading my legs slightly, giving him better access. He immediately takes advantage, his fingers finding my slick, sensitive flesh.

"*Fuck*, you're wet," he murmurs. "Let me make you come."

I can only nod, my breath coming in quick bursts. His

fingers move expertly, stroking and teasing, driving me higher and higher. I feel the tension inside me building, threatening to explode.

"Dax," I moan, clutching at the thin polyester bedspread. "Please… Don't stop."

He doesn't. He keeps touching me, stroking and caressing until I can't take it anymore.

"Yes, baby," he whispers roughly against my ear, then bites my neck.

I see stars. Fireworks. Whatever cliché fits the collapse of a carefully constructed universe. I cry out, back bowed, and he doesn't stop until I'm completely limp and trembling.

Dax runs his hands all over me. "Kendra," he says, his voice barely above a whisper. "I'm falling for you."

In the silence that follows, the ice machine down the hall drops a crushed load. Somewhere, a car backfires.

I wait for the fear. The panic. But neither comes.

Just the terrible, thrilling truth:

I'm falling for him, too.

CHAPTER 6
DAX

K endra turns to face me, her sapphire eyes wide. "I feel the same way, Dax."

Her words detonate in my chest.

I don't think—just turn her around and crush my mouth to hers.

Kendra moans into the kiss, her fingers tangling in my beard. It's a deep, soulful kiss, full of the promise of more. Her tongue slides against mine, hungry and demanding, and I hold her close, as if she might run away. But she arches into me, the damp heat of her still-trembling body searing through my shorts.

"*Fuck,* you taste good," I growl against her lips, palming her ass and dragging her closer. My cock throbs, trapped against her thigh.

She bites my lower lip, sharp and sweet. "You taste good, too. So good that I want to taste *more* of you."

Her hands grab my shirt, yanking it over my head.

Then she tugs at my waistband, nails scraping my hips. "Off."

I stand, pulling my shorts and boxers down together. Her gaze rakes over my body, lingering on my cock, thick and leaking. Her tongue darts out, wetting her lips.

Christ.

She crawls toward me, looking like sin in that borrowed shirt, and wraps her hand around my shaft. I hiss, hips jerking.

"You're huge," she says, wide-eyed.

Her fingers swipe over the head, spreading my precum, and I nearly black out. "Kendra—"

"Lie back." She pushes my chest and I collapse onto the mattress, my pulse skyrocketing. She straddles my thighs and rips off that fucking shirt, lifting up enough that I can see her beautiful pussy. Then she moves down my body, trailing kisses over my jaw and neck.

"Baby," I warn, my voice a low rumble. I'm already squirming. She continues her descent, her lips and tongue exploring every ridge and valley of my chest and abs.

I'm writhing like crazy as she moves over my hips, her breath hot on my skin. Her tongue flicks out, licking off the slickness beading at my tip. I buck, a low growl escaping me.

She smiles, eyes locked on mine, and takes me into her mouth. I nearly choke at the feel of her, so hot and wet.

"Jesus," I pant, one hand fisting the flimsy bedspread, the other tangling in her hair. Her tongue swirls around the tip before she sinks deeper, taking me to the root. She teases me, bringing me to the edge and then backing off only to do it all over again.

"You're driving me crazy, woman," I growl, my voice filled with desperation.

She hums, vibrating around me, and my hips tremble. Her nails dig into my thighs, holding me down as she sucks harder, faster.

I'm *dying* in the best possible way. Sweat drips down my neck as my balls tighten—

"Stop." I squeeze her shoulder, panting hard. "Need to be inside you. Please."

She smirks and climbs up, straddling my hips, her pussy hovering over my cock. "Begging already, are we?"

Her laugh is sweet and velvety, and I love hearing it.

"Wait. Should I go get protection?" I ask, cursing myself for not thinking of it sooner.

She shakes her head. "I'm on the pill, and I've been tested recently. You?"

"I'm not on the pill, but have been tested," I deadpan.

"Well, that settles that." She purses her lips, and our gazes lock. With a flex of her hips, she slides down, a slow impalement that has us both quivering. She's tight around me, velvety and warm. I close my eyes, relishing the feel of her, the heat—the squeeze of her muscles and the way she sighs, low and breathy, like I'm exactly where she needs me to be.

"Dammit," I groan. "You feel incredible."

"Fuck, Dax," she moans, her hips beginning to move. I grip her ass, my fingers digging into her flesh as I guide her up and down. She rides me hard and fast, her breath coming in quick gasps.

"That's it, baby," I encourage, my voice strained. "Ride me. Take everything you want."

Her head flies back. "Yes—"

"Look at me." I grip her waist. "Want to see you come again."

She rocks against me, grinding deep, her nails scoring my chest. "Harder, Dax."

"You asked for it," I moan as I flip us, pinning her beneath me. Her legs lock around my waist as I thrust hard into her, the slap of skin on skin echoing in the shitty motel room. She claws at my back, chanting my name, her full, round tits bouncing with every thrust.

"*Mine*," I snarl, biting her shoulder. "This pussy's all *mine*."

"Yes—fuck, Dax, all yours—"

Her heels dig into my ass, pulling me deeper. I lose my rhythm, fucking her raw, chasing that sweet friction. Her moans ratchet higher, louder.

"Come for me, Kendra," I demand, changing my angle.

Suddenly she cries out, shattering under me, and I watch her come undone. I follow her over the edge, spilling inside her with a broken cry.

Claiming her as my own.

We collapse in a sweaty heap, limbs tangled together. Kendra traces the ink on my chest, her breath warm against my skin.

"You're quiet," she eventually murmurs.

"Mm. Thinking about tomorrow."

Her hand stills. "I'm not backing out."

I catch her wrist, pressing her palm to my racing heart. "Viper's dangerous. I can't just—"

"You *can*." She pulls my face toward her, her gaze fierce. "I'm not some fragile thing, Dax. You need to trust me on this."

"I do." I cup her face, thumb brushing her lip. "But if he hurts you—"

She kisses me, soft and lingering. "You'll be there. I know."

I roll us over, tucking her against my chest. She fits perfectly, her perfect ass snug against my half-hard cock.

"Sleep," I mutter. "We'll figure it out in the morning."

She drifts off first, her breath evening out. I stare at the water-stained ceiling, inhaling her scent.

Fuck. I'm in deep.

As I drift off, I realize there's no way I can let her go through with this. I'm not sure how I'll convince her, but I have to find another way to get the evidence we need to clear my name. It's too risky.

She's *mine.*

And I'll burn this town down before I let Viper touch her.

CHAPTER 7
KENDRA

Dax's arm is still around my waist when I wake, his breath warm against my neck. For one blissful minute, I let myself melt into him—enjoy the steady beat of his heart, the scratch of his beard, the way his fingers twitch against my hip, as if he *needs* to touch me, even in sleep.

Then I remember.

Viper. The plan. The goddamn evidence.

I shift carefully, but his grip tightens. "No," he growls, still only half-awake, nuzzling my shoulder. "Stay."

"It's morning," I say, peeling his arm off. It stings worse than I want to admit. "We need to talk about tonight."

His eyes snap open, cognac swirling into stone. "No. *We* don't."

I grit my teeth. "Not this caveman routine again. The plan's solid. Viper's just dying to spill. He wants to impress me. All I need is twenty minutes in that motel room—"

"He's not some small-time crook, Kendra. He's a lethal snake who'll strike if he smells weakness." He sits up, the bed creaking, the sheets falling to his waist. "I'll find another way. Break into his shop, tear apart the bike myself—"

"And destroy the evidence in the process? Plus get arrested? Brilliant." I jam my legs into yesterday's latex pants, my skin still abuzz from the memory of his hands on me. "This is my job, Dax, and I'm damn good at it. You hired me to win, right? So *let me win*."

He stands abruptly, all six-foot-seven of furious muscle blocking the door to the bathroom. "Not with you as bait."

"You can't *forbid* me," I snap, toe-to-toe with him, tipping my chin up to glare daggers at him.

His jaw twitches. "Why not? You're mine to protect."

The words hang between us. I clench my fists. "No. You don't get to play the protective alpha male right now. You can either help me or stay out of my way. I'm not yours to command."

His face falls, and I know I've hurt him. But I was just trying to make a point.

I push past him into the bathroom, and the motel door slams a minute later.

When I come back out, he's gone.

The day passes in a blur of tension. Dax keeps his distance, his expression stony whenever our gazes meet. I do my best to focus on preparing for my rendezvous with Viper, ignoring the dull ache in my chest.

The rally throbs with energy, but I barely notice. I've been playing Viper all day—laughing at his jokes, brushing his arm, ignoring his bourbon breath. Dax shadows me like a storm cloud, jaw set, eyes pulling to murderous slits every time Viper's hands stray.

At sunset, I head to Viper's motel room, heart racing.

"Well, hey there, sexy lady," he purrs, his sleazy grin widening as he takes me in.

I force a smile, stepping inside. The room is a mess, with clothes and empty beer cans scattered across the floor. I try not to wrinkle my nose at the twin smells of tobacco and stale sweat. Then I notice some paperwork stuffed haphazardly in a bag near the small table.

Play the role, Kendra. Flirt, sweet-talk him, and then collect what you need.

Viper pours two whiskeys, his rat-tail practically twitching. "To new, hot friends," he says, leering and clinking my glass.

He sits down on the bed, patting the spot beside him invitingly. I perch on the edge, keeping a safe distance.

I giggle—*giggle!* How mortifying—and lean forward, letting my top gape open. "And to clever schemers. Nothing sexier than a man who...*bends* the rules, know what I mean?" I giggle again.

God, just shoot me now.

He preens, slicking his hair back with one hand. I'm sure his palm is a greasy mess. "Like the lawsuit I planted on that McCafferty schmuck? Yeah, that was pure genius. Will cost him a fortune in bad press and ruin his reputation. Plus, once he pays up, the bike's mine for parts."

Bingo. Glad I hit record on my phone before I came in. "Impressive," I purr. "How'd you do it?"

His smirk turns smug. "Bribed a rookie mechanic to swap the brake lines after delivery. Flimsy copper instead of steel. Super easy to cut. One sharp turn and—*boom.*" He mimes an explosion.

Got you, you slimy bastard.

I fake a swoon. "So smart. But wouldn't the copper be traceable?"

"Not when it's shredded to shit in a crash." He leans closer, sweat and cheap cologne choking me. "Enough shop talk. Let's get...*comfortable*." His hand slides up my thigh. "You're fucking hot, you know."

He blatantly stares at my cleavage, then his mouth lands on mine, sloppy and aggressive.

Barf. Will definitely be washing my mouth out with bleach later.

I pull back, breathless. "Bathroom first. Don't wanna... interrupt our fun later."

He chuckles, swatting my ass. "Hurry back, baby."

In the bathroom, I check my phone for the audio and save it, sending it to Dax too, just to be safe. I flush the toilet and take a deep breath before heading back out.

"Your turn," I say when I exit, batting my eyelashes and letting my hand drift down his skinny body toward his belt buckle.

He bites his lip. "Rowr," he says, then closes the bathroom door behind him.

I hustle over to his bag, pull out some of the papers and snap photos of anything that looks relevant—dates, part numbers, his sloppy signature proving that it was he who ordered the faulty lines. My hands shake, but triumph sings in my veins.

Dax's reputation is safe. I did it.

The toilet flushes as I rush to the front door, then I hear Viper growl and come up fast behind me.

I yelp as he grabs me, a sharp point pressed to my neck. "Where you goin?" he spits against my cheek.

"I was just going to grab a friend to join us—"

I feel the blade hovering by my throat. "Lying whore."

My adrenaline surges. I remember what Mitch taught me when I was twelve and slam my elbow into Viper's ribs. He grunts, his grip loosening as my boot crushes his instep.

"Bitch!" He lunges for me, the blade flashing. White-hot pain sears my arm.

The door splinters open as Dax kicks it in before he charges in, his expression feral, Kyle hot on his heels. Viper swings the knife but Dax catches his wrist, twisting until I hear the sickening sound of bone cracking.

Viper crumples, howling, and Dax's fist meets his jaw with another crunch. Viper falls to the ground, out cold.

"Kendra—" Dax reaches for me, eyes wild.

Blood soaks my sleeve, but I'm able to grin. "I got it. We won."

Then I plummet into darkness mid-smirk.

Beeps. Antiseptic. Dax's rough voice, anguished, "Please be okay, sweetheart."

I blink awake in the ER, the fluorescent lights hurting my eyes. My arm throbs and Dax's head is bent over my bed.

"Hi," I croak, surprised by my scratchy voice.

He jerks up, fixing me with bloodshot eyes. "God, don't ever scare me like that again."

"Oh—okay." I try to chuckle, but it comes out more like a wheeze.

He huffs, pressing his forehead to mine. "We got your recording. Just need those photos and we're golden. Oh, and *someone*—by which I mean, *Kyle*," he coughs, "called in a tip to the cops and they already raided Viper's shop. He and his crew are *super fucked*."

Relief floods me. "Told you I'm good."

"Too good." His thumb traces my cheek. "Listen, I owe you an apology. For trying to tell you what to do. You're a damn warrior, Kendra, and I'm just going to have to deal with it." He eyes my bandaged arm. "Just go easy on the war wounds, will ya?"

I smile. "I did what I had to do," I say. "I had to fight for justice. Fight for *you*."

He brushes my lip tenderly. "You're incredible."

"Right back at ya, Dax." I glance around. "Now, kiss me."

And he does…slowly, deeply, until my toes curl.

"Come live with me," he finally murmurs against my lips. "In Deepwood. Let's build a life that's half-courtroom, half-garage. I need you with me."

I sigh. "That sounds perfect. Because as it turns out, I need you with me, too."

And his chuckle rumbles through me, warm and certain.

EPILOGUE - DAX

ONE YEAR LATER

I tug at the goddamn bowtie. Fucking thing feels like it's choking me. I've worn suits before, but a *tuxedo*? This is a whole other level of torture. But for Kendra, I'd do anything—even dress up in a penguin suit and mingle with a bunch of uppity lawyers.

The city's fancy-ass legal gala is about as far as you can get from Deepwood Mountain, with crystal chandeliers, marble floors, and enough tuxes and gowns to make my eyes glaze over. Everywhere I look, there's some silver-haired shark in a thousand-dollar suit eyeing me like I'm a pee stain on their Persian rug.

But then I see Kendra.

She glides through the crowd in a floor-length shimmery blue dress that clings to every lethal curve, her hair spilling in waves over her shoulders like dark silk. She's holding a champagne flute, laughing at some suit's joke, but then her gaze flicks to me—*always* to me—and her smile turns private, wicked. My chest tightens.

She's mine.

A waiter glides up with a tray of tiny food that wouldn't satisfy a sparrow. "Caviar blini, sir?"

I grunt. "Got a burger hidden under that napkin?"

His expression doesn't change as Kendra appears like a vision, plucking a blini off the tray. "He'll have three," she says, pressing them into my palm. Her thumb brushes over my pulse point, and I swear the room gets ten degrees hotter.

"Surviving?" she murmurs.

"Barely." I pop a blini into my mouth. Tastes like salt and regret. "How's my tie?"

"A little crooked." She adjusts it, her fingers lingering. "But my goodness, you clean up well, Mr. Thomas. Almost didn't recognize you without the oil stains."

It's been a year since that shitty motel and Viper's downfall. A year of Kendra kicking ass in Deepwood, transforming the legal landscape in the town and beyond, making a name for herself and earning respect from even the toughest old-timers.

We've been married for two incredible months, and every day I fall deeper in love with her. She's my rock, my heart... my everything.

Mitch and Penny are over the moon that Kendra's stayed in Deepwood. Penny's pregnant, glowing and talking non-stop about baby names. Kendra's been a huge help, even offering to throw Penny a baby shower.

But tonight, it's all about my wife. She's receiving an award for her outstanding pro bono work, and I couldn't be prouder of her.

The emcee calls her up to present her with the award, and the room erupts. I clap loudest, my chest swelling as she takes the stage. She talks about justice and fighting for the little guy, her voice steady as a heartbeat.

That's my wife. The woman who took down Viper with a

phone recording, photos, and balls of steel—or maybe in this case, ovaries.

Later, when the music starts, I lead her to the dance floor. She raises a skeptical eyebrow. "You dance?"

I smirk. "Mom taught me a few moves." I slide a hand down her back, settling low on her waist. "She made me learn for the sake of 'future wife happiness'. Guess she knew something I didn't."

We begin to sway, slowly and easily. Kendra melts against me, her heat searing through my shirt. Her perfume—something expensive and dangerous—threatens to wreck my self-control.

Then I feel it.

No panties.

My grip tightens. *"Kendra…"*

She blinks up at me, all innocence. "Yes, my love?"

"You're…" I just shake my head.

Her lips curve. "Oh. You noticed."

I groan, my cock swelling against her hip. "You're trying to kill me, aren't you?"

"I'm trying to *thank* you." She grinds subtly, and I nearly trip over my feet. "For wearing the tux. For being there for me. For…everything."

Fuck. This woman.

I spin her, dipping her low enough to make her gasp. "You're playing with fire, wife."

"I know." Her eyes glitter. "But maybe I want to get burned."

The music shifts to something slower and sexier. I pull her close, my mouth at her ear. "Gotta find a secluded spot. Get this dress up around your waist. Lick your sweet pussy until you scream."

She shivers. "But the garden's closed. Gate's locked."

"You think I don't know how to pick a lock? Let's go."

Her laugh is breathless as I drag her through a side door. The night air slaps us, cool and sharp. We find the locked gate and I just kick the rusted thing right open.

The garden's all shadows and tangled roses, moonlight bathing the stone benches. I back her up against a trellis, kissing her hard. She moans, clawing at me as I grind against her.

I drop to my knees, hiking up her dress. She's bare, glistening, her thighs trembling. "Fuck, look at you. All soaked for me."

"Dax—please—"

I lick her slowly, savoring each gasp. She winds her hands through my hair, urging me on. I tease and suck at her clit relentlessly until her legs begin to shake.

"That's it, baby. Come on my tongue."

She arches, a broken cry tumbling out, and I drink her down, my cock aching.

As she sags against the trellis, I stand, wiping my mouth. "Round two's in the limo. Let's roll."

She grabs my belt, yanking me close. "Dax, wait."

I'm about to argue when she presses my hand to her stomach.

"I'm pregnant."

The world stops.

Pregnant.

"Already?" She just stopped taking the pill last month.

She shrugs. "Guess you have strong swimmers."

A kid. *Our* kid. A tiny hellion with her brains and my stubbornness.

I crush her to me, kissing her until we're both dizzy. "Best fucking news," I rasp against her lips.

89

I scoop her up, carrying her toward the lights. "We're still finishing what we started, though. Gotta celebrate *thoroughly.*"

She nips my earlobe. "Home. Now."

Thank god for the limo's tinted windows. We barely make it inside before she's straddling me, her dress hiked up, my tux in ruins. I sink into her, both of us gasping.

"I love you," she whispers, riding me slowly.

I grip her hips, my heart full. "Love you more, Mrs. Thomas."

Later, as we lie tangled together in bed at the house—her head on my chest, my hand splayed over her still-flat stomach —I trace the scar on her arm that she earned fighting for me.

"You're my hero, you know," I murmur.

She smiles sleepily. "Right back at you, big guy."

The future's wide open. Courtroom? Garage? Nursery? Doesn't matter.

Wherever she is, that's home.

FILTHY FIX

CHAPTER 1
ELLIE

A shiny bell above the door jingles as I step out of the sweltering summer heat and into the cool office space of McCafferty Customs.

Thank god this shop has decent AC.

I scan the reception area.

It's clean and welcoming, decorated in (you guessed it) a biker theme.

Framed photos of celebrities and their motorcycles adorn the walls, along with vintage bike posters and surprisingly tasteful pin-up art in a variety of shiny chrome frames. There's a black couch off to one side, made of what seems to be the same leather as a motorcycle jacket.

This place came highly recommended by motorcycle enthusiasts all over the web and since I live pretty close to Deepwood Mountain, I figured I'd give them a shot.

As I approach the counter, my worn leather boots tap against the concrete floor. A woman rushes into the office from the back with a warm smile and a loose, tawny bun. "Hi there, welcome to McCafferty Customs! I'm Lily. How can we help you today?"

"I'd like to get an estimate for repairing this bike," I say, nodding towards the trailer hitched to my SUV outside the window.

She gazes outside. "Sweet ride! We'll have a look. You mind if we take it off the trailer, Ms.—?"

"Just Eloísa," I reply. "Actually, Ellie, is best. And do whatever you need to do."

Lily nods. "Have a seat, Ellie, and I'll come grab you." Then she turns to head out to the garage. "Zane!" she calls, disappearing.

I sit down on the couch and watch out the window as a big, muscled, guy with dark hair and tats—who I assume is Zane—removes the bike from the trailer and rolls it away.

Moments later, Lily returns. "Come on back."

I follow her into the garage just as the phone rings.

"Hang tight," she says. "Kyle will be over shortly." She runs off to grab the phone.

The chrome fender of my ex-husband's 1972 Harley Sportster winks at me under the garage lights like it's in on some cosmic joke.

His baby, *my* cross to bear.

The engine's been dead for two years, about as long as our marriage managed to sputter along before choking on our contempt. But now it's my ticket to freedom and a new beginning.

I squat down to look at the rusted exhaust pipe and trail a finger over the dusty seat, half expecting it to hiss at me.

"You here to resurrect the beast or bury it?"

The voice is all honey and gravel, and it comes attached to a pair of grease-stained work boots sauntering into my periphery. I look up—*way* up—and nearly drop my purse clutched to my chest.

Oh. My.

The man is a walking contradiction to every buttoned-up CEO type I used to orbit around in my past life as a marketing executive. A faded bandana holds back sun-kissed hair, sleeves of tattoos peek out from under rolled-up flannel, and a grin that could thaw Montana in January spreads across his face. His name's stitched on his vintage mechanic's uniform shirt: *Kyle*.

"Depends." I stand up and square my shoulders, channeling the icy poise that used to make junior associates cry. "How much will it cost to make it someone else's problem?"

He chuckles, low and warm, and crouches to inspect the bike. The movement pulls his jeans taut over thighs that could crack walnuts.

Heavens.

He runs his hands over the sleek frame with a reverence that borders on sensual. "She's a beauty. But crankshaft's probably rusted to hell," he says, peering at the engine. "Carbs are shot. Tires bald as my Uncle Larry." I'm transfixed by his fingers—broad and calloused. "But her bones are good. With enough time and cash, she'll purr."

I dig my nails into my palms. "Define 'enough cash.'"

He stands, wiping his hands on a rag, and fixes me with slate-blue eyes that crinkle at the corners. "Three grand. Minimum."

My stomach plummets. I can't afford that if I'm only going to make a profit of two to three grand when I sell it. I need every penny for the taqueria: the dream I've scribbled in notebooks since *Abuela* let me roll my first tamale at six. The one that my ex, Ben, bulldozed over when I brought it up a year ago.

Kyle leans against a tool chest, all relaxed confidence. "You plan on selling the bike then?"

I nod. "It's my ex husband's bike. He left it with me in the divorce. And now I need the money. But I can't sink that much into repairs. I've done my research and I won't get enough back on the sale."

"Hold on." Kyle straightens up. "I thought you ladies kept the ring, not the chopper."

I can't help but laugh at his bewilderment, and it feels good to let the tension ease a bit. "Let's just say I'd rather turn *this* into cash and start my own business than wear a ring that reminds me of the worst decision of my life." I huff. "And well, the bike's worth a lot more than the ring was."

His eyebrows shoot up, and he lets out a low whistle. "Damn. You're fierce. I like it."

I bite back a smile.

Kyle tilts his head, scratching the stubble along his jaw. "How about we barter then."

"Barter?" Wow, this really *is* a small town.

He shrugs. "I have a good feeling about you. I'm sure we can negotiate a deal."

"Why do you say that?"

He chuckles. "Vibes. And well, observation." He taps his temple. "Like how you've glanced at my arms six times since I walked over. Not that I'm counting."

Heat floods my face. "You're—"

"Charming? Devastatingly handsome?"

"Annoying," I lie. *Mostly.* He *is* annoying—annoyingly attractive *and* annoyingly right.

He grins, unrepentant.

"Fine. Let's barter. I mean, I don't know how else I'm going to get the money to rent restaurant space in Helena."

"What kind of restaurant?"

"A taqueria."

He clutches at his chest. "You're teasing me, right? Did Remi put you up to this?"

"Who's Remi?"

He blinks and his expression turns thoughtful. "I'll tell you what. You bring me dinner here every night for the next two weeks, I'll fix this baby up for half the cost."

This time I blink at him, taken aback. "What?" He wants food? "You're serious?"

He nods. "Dead serious. I love Mexican food, and I never turn down a home-cooked meal." He steps closer, the scent of motor oil and spearmint gum invading my space. "It's *all* good — from *carne asada* tacos, *enchiladas verdes*, to that melty Oaxaca stuff that makes a man reconsider his life choices."

My traitorous brain conjures *Abuela's* recipe for *chiles en nogada,* and me licking cream sauce off his—

No.

I back up, hitting the bike's handlebar.

His gaze drops to my lips. "So I've got a weakness for complicated women and good *queso.*"

A laugh bursts out of me, sharp and unexpected. "I'm *not* complicated." *Right?*

"Sure." He gestures to the Harley. "Just a gal selling her ex's bike to fund a culinary revolution. Simple as pie."

The truth scrapes me raw. *Ben's sneer when I mentioned the taqueria. The way he'd roll his eyes if I suddenly got ideas for potential menu items or gasped when I saw a vacant space that looked perfect.* I swallow hard. "What's the catch?"

"No catch." He shrugs. "I'm a patriot supporting local cuisine. Plus—" he nods toward the shop office, where a woman with neon green streaks in her black hair is arguing with another burly mechanic "—Remi keeps stealing my lunch."

Silence stretches on, thrumming with the buzz of grinders and the pulse in my ears. *They'd be business transactions. Not dates. Just dinner.*

The ghost of Ben's condescension rasps in my ear: *You'll fail. You always do.*

I thrust out my hand. "You're on. Two weeks of dinners."

Kyle's palm engulfs mine, warm and rough against my skin. "Bad *ass*." He doesn't let go. "Lily said your name's Ellie right?"

I nod.

"Well, Ellie, I'll get to work on this bike. And I'll see you tomorrow."

"Six okay?"

"Perfect." He's still holding my hand as he winks. "Until then, *mi reina*."

My queen. The Spanish zings through me, reigniting the blush I've been fighting. He saunters off, whistling, and I press my cold hands to my cheeks.

Soy una idiota.

CHAPTER 2
KYLE

I've rebuilt engines at three a.m. with a concussion and frostbitten fingers. But I've never struggled to focus like I am right now.

Her smile keeps replaying in my head, sharp and bright as a spark plug igniting. She'd muttered something in Spanish under her breath yesterday, cheeks pink as sunset, and I find myself wishing I knew more Spanish.

The Harley sits in my bay, a dusty relic of a past Ellie seems desperate to leave behind. I wonder about the ex who left her with this bike and a heart full of scars.

What kind of man lets go of a woman like her?

Time ticks by, and the bike begins to reveal its secrets. I was right in my original assessment—carbs shot, crankshaft rusted —but there's hope for the frame. These classics are strong. With enough time and care, it'll be a stunner.

Just like Ellie.

"You're grinnin' like a possum eatin' persimmons," Dax says, tossing a rag at my head.

I catch it mid-air without looking up from the Harley's rusted guts.

"I bet it's that new smoke show of a lady friend you got."

I stiffen. The *crunch* of my ratchet tightening echoes too loud. "She's a *customer*." Though yes, I wouldn't mind if she were more. I just don't want to give Dax the satisfaction that he's right.

Remi saunters over, a titanium fastener clenched between her teeth like a cigar. She pulls it out briefly. "You gave her a *'fix your bike for tacos'* deal. For you, that's like sliding into her DMs."

I roll my eyes. "It's strategic community support."

"Strategic *dick* support," Zane grunts walking in from the office.

They all erupt into obnoxious laughter. Typical. I flip them off, but my chest feels weirdly tight. Ellie's not just some random woman. There's a current under her concrete-wall exterior—something wounded and ferocious that makes me want to tear down every brick between us with my teeth.

The rest of the crew leaves for the day, and I'm left elbow-deep in grease when I hear a van door slide closed and little sneakers slapping concrete.

"Uncle Kyle!"

Evan, my nephew, barrels into my legs, his Spider-Man backpack smacking my thigh.

"Evan!" My sister yells. "What did we tell you about running into the shop? You need to wait for me. It's dangerous!"

I get up from under the bike and give him a stern look.

"Sorry," he says, burying his face in my pant leg.

"It's okay, bud," I say, ruffling his blond hair. "Just be more careful next time."

Juniper appears, shaking her head. Delilah, her newest baby, babbles from her hip, reaching chubby fists toward me.

Sis looks exhausted in that glowing mom way, her ponytail lopsided.

"Emergency visit," she says, coming over to plop Delilah into my arms. "This monster," she nods at Evan, who's now trying to reassemble my socket set, "told his teacher I'm a police siren."

"Accurate." I bounce Delilah, breathing in her baby powder smell. "You're loud and nosey."

Juniper swats me. "He demonstrated with Daddy's 'WEOWEOWEO' during silent reading time."

My sister works as a dispatcher for the Sheriff's Department, and her husband, Isaac is the sheriff.

"Genius," I deadpan. "Harvard's gonna fight MIT for him."

My ears perk up when I hear the sound of a car door slam.

Ellie walks into the garage holding a stainless steel catering tray like a warrior queen with a shield. Her dark hair's loose today, curling wild around her shoulders. My mouth waters... for multiple reasons.

"Right on time," I say, suddenly giddy.

She freezes when she spots Juniper. "Oh. I didn't realize you had..."

"A hostage situation?" Juniper rescues Delilah from gnawing my bandana. "I'm Juniper. Kyle's sister and professional wrangler of tiny terrorists. Named Evan and Delilah." She points to my nephew and niece.

Ellie's obvious relief and cautious smile unravels me. "Oh, hi. I'm Ellie. And I brought plenty of food, so please have some." She sets the tray on my workbench.

The aroma of spices and grilled meat fill the air. I lean in, inhaling deeply. "Man, that smells amazing."

Evan scrambles onto a stool, eyeing the food. "Is there candy?"

"I think this is better," Ellie says, lifting the lid.

The scent hits me first—ginger-lime *carne asada*, charred onions, cilantro. My stomach growls like the Sportster's busted engine.

"You're welcome to have some, if your mom says it's okay." Ellie looks between Evan and Juniper.

"Can I, Mom?" he asks, with a smile, then glances at my sister.

Juniper nods and holds up her finger. "One."

"These are *tacos de carne asada*," Ellie says, putting some meat in a corn tortilla with some *pico de gallo* then handing it to Evan. "It's marinated steak."

"*Awesome!*" Evan takes it and chomps down, sauce smeared across his cheeks. "Tastes like dinosaurs!"

Ellie laughs, genuine and warm, and I swear the fluorescent lights sparkle.

She waggles her eyebrows at Evan. "Next week, I'll bring brains."

"Brains?" Evan's eyes widen. "So I can be like a zombie?"

"Yep, *tacos de sesos*. They're delicious." She grins at Evan and makes a few tacos and hands them to me and Juniper nodding toward the salsas and limes for us to use.

"Oh, you've done it now. He'll be your best friend forever," Juniper says, then takes a bite of her taco. She blinks. "And you're *definitely* my favorite person now. *Yum!*"

Ellie's grins. "I'm glad you like them."

I finally bite into mine. *Holy hell.* The meat's buttery, smokey, and has the perfect texture. And the tomatillo salsa has to be the best I've ever had. So bright and herby. A moan slips out.

Ellie's gaze snaps to me. "Good?"

I hurriedly make myself another. "I might propose."

"That doesn't surprise me," Juniper adds. "This guy loves his Mexican food."

Ellie rolls her eyes, but color floods her cheeks. "It's just meat, tortillas, and a few toppings."

"No downplaying it. This is a *religious experience.*" I step closer, lowering my voice. "You trying to ruin me for all other women?"

Her throat moves as she swallows, and I'm dying to kiss her right there.

Dammit.

Our eyes lock, and the air hums like a live wire.

Then a lime wedge flies in between us and the spell breaks.

"Evan!" Juniper exclaims.

He giggles and I turn to grab him, tickling his sides. "You little—"

He squeals and Delilah laughs in Juniper's arms.

Saved by the troublemaker.

"Please tell me you're opening a restaurant," Juniper asks.

Ellie's shoulders tense. "I plan on opening a taqueria...if I can secure funding."

"She's selling this old girl to help pay for it," I jump in, patting the Sportster. And a piece falls off.

We all look at the rusted metal now on the ground.

"It just needs...the right hands to fix it," Ellie says, the reverence in her tone punching my gut.

As we eat, Ellie watches Juniper and the kids, a wistful look in her eyes. I wonder what she's thinking, what dreams she's chasing. I want to know more about her, about the life she left behind and the one she's building now.

Evan, his face smeared with taco sauce, looks up at Ellie with wide eyes. "Can you teach me to make tacos?"

Ellie laughs, ruffling his hair. "Of course, kiddo. But you've got to promise to eat them all."

Evan grins, holding up his pinky. "Deal."

Ellie hooks her pinky around his, shaking on it. The gesture is small, but it sends a warmth spreading through me. She's a natural with kids, her eyes lighting up with a genuine affection that's hard to fake.

"Well, we gotta go." Juniper frowns at her phone. "Naptime meltdown incoming in 3...2..."

Delilah wails on cue and Ellie begins hustling to pack some into a container. "Take some home. *Please.*"

"You'll be my husband's favorite person now, too." Juniper laughs. "You're definitely catering my PTA meetings," Juniper says, taking the container. "Thank you!"

I kiss Delilah on the head and squeeze Evan before giving him a push.

"Bye!" Ellie waves as Juniper herds Evan toward the van. Her smile falters as she watches them leave, a hollow look in her eyes. I take note of it.

"Smart, doing the dinner trade," she says, too brightly. "Feeding you *and* bribing your family."

I lean against the workbench, our hips inches apart. "You're not the first to try winning me over with food."

"I'm not trying to win you over. I'm paying for your service," she replies, but her cheeks are pink.

"Well, Remi left a dead rat in my toolbox last Valentine's Day."

Ellie snorts. "Romantic."

"I prefer your style." I move my hand closer to hers. "*Salsa verde* over rodents any day."

Her breath hitches when I skim my thumb over her knuckles.

The shop phone rings, making us both flinch.

"Ignore it," I murmur. "It's after hours."

She shakes her head and begins cleaning up. "I should go."

"Stay." The word slips out raw, desperate. "Help me tune the engine?" I quickly add.

There it is—that flash of yearning before her walls slam up.

"I've got recipes to test."

"Right." I walk her out, conscious of the space between us. Her SUV smells like charred meat, cinnamon, and limes.

"*Hasta mañana, mi reina*," I say.

"Goodnight, Kyle," she says, chuckling as she drives off.

Back in the garage, I inhale the rest of the tacos, savoring the burn of the *salsa rojo*.

I imagine the taste of Ellie's mouth is just as spicy.

Yeah, I need more tacos.

And then a cold shower.

CHAPTER 3
ELLIE

By the fifth evening, I've started to look forward to six p.m. like it's a holy hour.

I stride into the McCafferty Customs garage balancing a tray of *chiles rellenos* and fresh tortillas, the scent of roasted poblanos clinging to my hair.

Kyle is sprawled beneath the Harley, humming a country song, his boot tapping the concrete floor in rhythm. I'm suddenly aware of the way his denim-clad hips and thighs flex as he adjusts his position.

"D-delivery for *el gordo*," I call out, setting the food on Kyle's workbench. I can say this because the man is *all* lean muscle. Though I have no idea how with all the food he can put away.

"One sec, *mi reina*. Just gotta..." The ratchet in his hand clangs. "There. *Now* I can properly worship you."

He slides out on the creeper, hair dusted with rust flakes, and pops up with a grin that should come with a warning label.

"Still not your queen," I reply, averting my eyes.

"Fine." He grins. "But you *are* the only woman who's ever handed me tools without chucking them at my head."

"Remi told me you deserved it last time."

His eyes travel down my body, his smudged cheeks and tousled hair doing unfair things to my pulse. "Remi's a snitch." Over the past few days we've settled into a rhythm: I arrive at dusk with a steaming dish—*tacos de sesos, tinga de pollo, mole negro*—and Kyle greets me with a quip and a warmth that chips away at my armor.

Sometimes others from the crew are still there and they sample my food as we chat, then they leave Kyle and I to it.

Typically, I hand him tools as he explains motorcycle parts like they're poetry, both of us pretending not to notice how often our fingers brush.

But tonight feels…charged. The garage is empty except for the hum of the fluorescent lights above and the groan of the industrial fan fighting July's wrath.

Kyle sits next to me on the bench seat and devours two *chiles rellenos* before groaning. "*Dios mío.* You sure you won't marry me?"

"Temporary partnerships only," I say lightly, picking at my food. "No lifetime contracts."

He grabs another helping, studying me. "Your ex really did a number on you, huh?"

The question catches me off guard, but I know Kyle doesn't mean to be harsh. He's not my ex. "Ben preferred a passive and obedient wife. I failed at both."

"That fucker's loss." Kyle's voice softens. "And the taqueria? How'd he feel about that?"

"He said I'd embarrass myself. That my 'little hobby' would flop faster than a soufflé in a thunderstorm." The memory tastes bitter, familiar.

Kyle snorts. "Man's a moron. You could sell ice in a blizzard with food like this."

A flush creeps up my neck. "Flattery won't get you extra guac."

"Not flattery. Fact." He wipes his mouth, gaze steady. "You ever think he was just scared?"

"Of *me*?"

"Hell yes. A woman who fights for what she wants? That's terrifying to some men—the insecure ones, at least."

The compliment lodges under my ribs, warm and dangerous.

We eat in comfortable silence until we hear a car pull up.

Juniper and the kids walk up. Evan blurts out, "Uncle Kyle! Mom says you gotta fix my bike!"

Kyle stands and scoops him up, dangling him upside down. "You wrecked it again?"

"I jumped it over a volcano!" Evan shrieks, giggling.

Juniper appears, a hand over her forehead, baby Delilah tucked under her other arm. "Sorry to interrupt. He wouldn't let up until we saw you both. And for the record, it was an *ant hill*, not a *volcano*." She chuckles, then nods at the Harley. "Progress?"

"Getting there," Kyle says, righting Evan. "Ellie's the real MVP. Keeps me from bolting the exhaust to the gas tank."

Juniper smirks. "I bet."

"Would you like some *chiles rellenos*?" I ask.

"We just had pizza with Daddy!" Evan says to me.

"Wow, how fun! I love pizza," I reply. "What toppings did it have?"

Evan takes a moment to think. "Peppowoni and sausage."

"Sounds delicious." I wink at him, then smile at Juniper.

I was surprised when Evan actually tried my *tacos de sesos* two days ago. He wasn't kidding about wanting to be a zombie the way he scarfed them down. The kid is definitely creative and adventurous. And I promised Juniper I'd come by on the weekend to show Evan how to make tacos as promised. Kyle said he'd come, too.

I smile to myself. I can't wait.

I'm excessively aware of Kyle's laugh rumbling through the garage as he helps fix Evan's bike. Of how he kneels to let Evan "help" tighten a bolt, guiding tiny hands with infinite patience.

When they leave, Kyle catches me staring. "What?"

"Nothing. Just…you're good with him."

He shrugs, but his ears turn pink. "Kids are easy. They either want candy or to conquer the world. They're not complicated like adults."

"Says the man who still eats Fruit Loops for dinner."

"Until you came along," he says, grinning.

I laugh, and his eyes darken.

He clears his throat. "C'mere. Wanna show you something."

I step closer, and he guides my hand to the bike's fuel line, his calloused palm over mine. "Feel that? Pulse is weak. Needs a better flow."

All I feel is the heat of his chest against my back, his breath skimming my ear. "Y-yeah."

"We'll replace the pump. But first…" He turns me to face him, our hands still linked. "You got any siblings?"

The question throws me. "A sister. Letty. She's in Portland."

"Close?"

"We were." I pick at a thread on my jeans to avoid gazing directly into his eyes. "Ben didn't like *sharing* me. By the time I filed for divorce, we'd…drifted."

Kyle's thumb strokes my wrist. "You'll fix it. Family's worth the fight."

It's the certainty in his voice that undoes me. That makes me whisper, "What about you? You and Juniper seem…"

"She's my heart," he says simply. "Took her in when she finally left our shitty parents. She met Isaac pretty darn quick, but she knows I'll stick with her through anything."

The raw love in his voice cracks something open in me. "She's lucky."

"Nah. I'm the lucky one." He leans in, our noses inches apart. "Just like I'm lucky you walked in here."

The world shrinks to the heat in his breath, the tiny flecks of gold in his blue eyes. My gaze drops to his mouth.

Bad idea. Bad idea. Bad—

But *he* kisses me.

It's not gentle. It's gasoline and fire, his lips claiming mine with a hunger that singes my doubts to ash. I fist his shirt, pulling him closer, and he growls low in his throat, backing me against the workbench. Something clatters to the floor as he lifts me onto it, slotting himself between my thighs.

His hands dive into my hair, tilting my head as he deepens the kiss, my mouth melting into his. I moan, and he swallows the sound, his stubble burning my chin.

When we break apart, gasping, he rests his forehead against mine. *"Fuck."*

Reality crashes back in. I push him away, heartbeat roaring. "This—this can't happen."

My lips tingle and my entire body is thrumming.

He steps back, chest heaving. "Why not?"

"Because I'm—"

"Brilliant? Stunning? The best goddamn kisser in Montana?"

"Older," I blurt the first thing that comes to mind. "I'm thirty-eight, Kyle. What are you…like twenty-five?"

He barks a laugh. "I'm twenty-eight. And *thirty-eight* is not a fossil."

"I've got ten years on you, Kyle!"

"And?" He cages me against the bench, eyes blazing. "You think I care about a silly number? I want *you*. The woman whose Spanish makes my cock throb. Who makes food that could end wars. Who's so scared of being happy, she'd rather hide behind her ex's bullshit than admit she's still alive and a total badass."

Tears prick my eyes. "You don't know what I've lost."

"Then let me help you find it again." His thumb swipes my cheek, gentle now.

"I should go," I say, and Kyle moves back, as I slide off the bench, knees wobbly.

He catches my wrist. "Stay. Let's talk."

Run, my brain screams. *Stay*, my heart counters.

"Tomorrow," I rasp, pulling free. "Same time?"

His thumb strokes my racing pulse once, twice, before he releases me. "Always."

The drive home is a blur and I lean into the curves of the mountain road, windows down, letting the cool air chill the flush off my skin.

You shouldn't have kissed him back.

But all I see is the reverence in Kyle's gaze as he called my ex scared. Of me! And all I feel is the brand of his palms on my body, the taste of his mouth on my lips.

That night, I dream of steel and spice and this man who threatens to undo me.

CHAPTER 4
KYLE

My brain counts down the hours until Ellie walks back through that garage door.

It's been three days since that kiss. The one that made me forget all other kisses—all other *women*—in an instant.

Since then she's avoided my eyes and handed me wrenches, screwdrivers, and other tools like they're ticking time bombs.

And it's been *hell* trying to pretend my cock isn't made of steel every time she leans over the Sportster's engine.

That said, I haven't let up on my flirting. Just because she said the kiss couldn't happen again, doesn't mean I'm going to stop letting her know how I feel about her.

But today's our first test ride on the bike.

I rev the Harley's engine, the growl rattling my molars. *Oh yeah, I'm good.* "Ready, *mi reina*?"

Ellie stands in the garage doorway, arms crossed, the setting sunlight haloing her wild dark hair. She licks her lips, and I track the movement like a goddamn bloodhound.

"It's not going to explode, is it?"

"Define *explode*." I toss her a helmet, grinning when she

rolls those whiskey eyes. "Not a chance." Now, there's a whole host of things that *could* happen, but hell if I'd take her out on a bike I didn't think was safe. "I had Zane triple-check everything we've done so far."

She seems satisfied with that and straps on the helmet, her fingers trembling just enough to make me want to pin her against the wall and kiss the fear away. Instead, I kick down the stand and pat the seat behind me.

"Rules of the road: Hold tight, lean when I lean, and don't bite my neck unless you mean it."

"You're *terrible.*" But she's smiling as she swings her leg over the bike—sweet Christ, *those jeans*—and slides up against me. Her thighs clamp around my hips, arms looping around my waist.

I rev the engine again. "Full disclosure, I named this bike."

She smacks my stomach. "Let's hear it."

"*Mariposa.* For that butterfly tattoo on your wrist."

The inhale at my neck tells me she's blushing.

We tear out of the garage, summer wind whipping around us. I grin, twisting the throttle, and the bike eats up the asphalt of the mountain road with ease. Ellie's grip tightens as we hit the mountain road, each curve pressing her closer, her heat bleeding through my jacket, and damn, if it doesn't feel right. Like she's meant to be here, riding with me. By the time we crest a hill and reach the overlook, I'm hard and dizzy.

Sunset paints the valley sprawled below in shades of green and gold as I kill the engine. Ellie yanks off her helmet, cheeks flushed, eyes lit up like the Fourth of July. "*Dios mío,* that was…"

"Better than cooking?" I hop off, offering a hand.

"Let's not get crazy here." She takes my hand, fingers lingering in mine.

We settle on a warm flat rock, the sides carved with tons of names, hearts, and other more vulgar doodles. She hugs her knees to her chest, looking out at the panorama, and I watch her, the way the sun catches her profile, the contentment softening her features.

"Where did you learn how to cook, anyway?" I ask, laying back on laced fingers.

"My *abuela*...my grandmother," she replies, eyes sparkling as she stretches her legs out, boots brushing my thigh.

She tells me about the summers she spent in Mexico with her grandmother, and I listen intently, drinking in every reverent word she has for that time in her life.

"Do you remember the first dish you ever made by yourself?" I ask.

A smile plays on her lips. "It was *arroz con leche*. Rice pudding. I must have been eight or nine, and I wanted to surprise my *abuela*. I ended up burning the rice and making a huge mess in the kitchen, but she loved it. She said it was the best *arroz con leche* she'd ever tasted."

I laugh. "I bet it was delicious."

She shakes her head. "Nope, it was *awful*." She laughs. "But she made me feel like I could do anything, like I was capable of greatness. That's what I want to do with my taqueria. I want to make people feel that way, like my food will give them a bit of her kindness, her encouragement to do anything after a good meal, as if they're part of something special."

I cover her hand with mine. "You will, Ellie. I have no doubt about it."

She turns and smiles at me, then nods toward the bike.

"By the way, you're not half bad at this mechanic stuff."

"Wait'll you see what else I'm good at." I wink.

"Hmm." Her smirk is lethal. "Barbecues? Yardwork? Meditation, maybe?"

"Naked yoga," I deadpan.

Her snort echoes across the canyon. "You'd pull a muscle."

"I'm surprisingly flexible." My thumb skims her knee. "Persistent, too."

Her breath stutters, gaze dropping to my mouth.

I swallow and tear my eyes away. *Damn,* I want to kiss her so badly.

But when I go to move away, her hand grabs the collar of my shirt.

She leans in and kisses *me.*

It starts soft—a question. One she never has to ask of *me.* I'll take this anytime, anywhere. My lips part under hers, and it's mesmerizing. She tastes of lime and spice. She runs her hands into my hair and I groan. Her nails scrape my scalp and *fuck,* I'm gone. I haul her on top of me, her legs straddling my hips as I lick into her mouth. She moans, grinding down, and I nearly come in my jeans right there.

A tremor runs through her. Tiny, but there. Her fingers clench my shoulders like she's clinging to a cliff edge.

Slow, my brain hisses through the lust fog. *She's scared.*

I break the kiss, holding her face in my hands. "Ellie."

"What?" she pants. "I'm fine."

"Liar." I brush her hair back, heart jackhammering. "You told me before that something like this couldn't happen again. I don't want you to do something you're not ready for. We've got time to figure this out. All the time you need."

She studies me, eyes searching. "How did—why are you—?"

"Because the first time I make you scream my name, I want you *sure.*"

She shivers, and nods. Then she rolls off me, to lie on her back.

I fight the urge to pull her back to me.

But we stay there as the sun sinks and the sky turns to

twilight, listening to the leaves rustling in the wind, and the birds singing their evening songs.

The ride back is slower, more relaxed, her warmth seeping into my bones. I'm getting addicted to this feeling—to her.

As we approach the garage, a sleek, black sedan pulls up.

I cut the engine and help Ellie off the bike, as a man decked out in a custom suit, patent-leather shoes, and a face like a pissed-off Ken doll, strides toward us.

"Ellie, what the *hell* is this?" he demands.

Ellie freezes, her smile dying.

"We're closed, sir," I say, crossing my arms, something primal in me wanting to shield her.

"What are you doing here, Ben?"

Ben? As in her ex? That explains it.

He jabs a finger at the Sportster. "I'm getting my bike back before you sell it. Probably for that ridiculous restaurant idea of yours, right?"

"*Your* bike?" Her voice could ice the Sahara. "Per our divorce settlement, I own everything in that garage. Including your midlife crisis. And I can do whatever the fuck I please with it."

Ben steps into the fluorescent light, reeking of expensive cologne and entitlement. "You're going to ruin it. Give it back or—"

"Or what?" I'm between them before I blink. "Call your therapist? Cry into your stock portfolio?" I huff. "You're awfully concerned about a bike you left to die in a pile of rusty metal."

He sneers, glancing at her. "Who's this? Your new grease-monkey?"

Ellie moves to my side. "He's my *business partner*. Who actually *knows* how engines work."

Ben's laugh grates like bad brakes. "Christ, Ellie—you upgraded to trailer trash? Couldn't even find a man your own age?"

Red floods my vision and I crack my knuckles. "I think you need to back off."

Ellie grabs my wrist. "Kyle, don't."

Ben smirks. "What? Is he gonna hit me? Bet Daddy taught you that between meth—"

CRACK

The metal shelving beside him rings as I punch it instead, avoiding the jerkoff's face by inches. He stumbles back, eyes wide, tripping over his own feet.

"Next time," I growl, looming over him, "I won't miss."

Ellie's hand slides into mine. "Leave, Ben. Before I let him finish."

He scrambles up, face purple. "I'm getting that bike back. You'll be hearing from my lawyer!" He strides to his car, slamming the door before driving off.

Ellie steps in front of me, studying my split knuckles. "You shouldn't have done that." She grabs a clean rag from the rack and wraps my hand in it.

"That guy deserves a real punch in the face."

She huffs a laugh, then presses her lips to my throbbing hand. "True. *Es un imbécil.*"

I smile. "You okay?"

"Better than okay." She pulls my hand up and rubs her cheek against it. "*He* doesn't get to hurt me anymore."

My chest tightens. Because *god*, she's magnificent. Because I'd do anything for her. To keep that fire in her eyes and protect her from the shadows of her past.

Because I'm in love with this woman.

CHAPTER 5
ELLIE

After Ben tears out of the parking lot, the adrenaline in my veins doesn't fade.

It *thrums*, hot and electric.

As Kyle flexes his bloody knuckles, all I can think about is how he stood up for me, defending me with unwavering loyalty and a growl that could intimidate even the toughest biker. He was ready to fight. And Ben deserved it for shooting his mouth off, calling Kyle those horrible things.

But Kyle didn't hit the bastard. He held back for *me*. The realization sears through me until my skin feels too tight, too warm.

"You might need some ice for that," I say, voice steadier than I feel.

"Ice can wait." He tosses the rag on the workbench.

"I'm sorry for...him," I say.

He moves closer, his hand brushing my hip. "Never apologize for that prick's behavior." His voice is gravel-rough and it sends a shiver crawling down my spine. I glance up, and his gaze locks onto mine like a tractor beam. His pupils are blown wide, chest heaving under his shirt. His raw protectiveness, the way he'd snarled at Ben like a feral wolf defending its mate, shouldn't make my thighs clench. But it does. *God*, it does.

Memories flash through my mind: Ben's sneer at my dreams, his dismissive laughter when I mentioned the taqueria. But Kyle? Kyle called my food a *religious experience.* He rebuilt my ex's junk-heap bike into something beautiful, just to help *me.*

I want this man.

I grab his face and crash my lips to his.

He freezes for a heartbeat—probably surprised—then groans into my mouth. The kiss is primal, all teeth and hunger, his tongue claiming mine as he backs me against the Harley. The bike's handlebar digs into my lower back, but I don't care. The pain only fuels the fire. The *need.*

"Ellie," he rasps against me, nipping at my throat. His voice is a wreck, rough and desperate. "You sure you want this?"

"Kyle, I want you to fuck me until we both can't think straight." The words tumble out of my mouth on one shaky breath and he sways as if I punched him.

"*Fuck,* you can't say things like that to me..." he shakes his head, as if coming to from a hit.

I smile and grab him by his belt buckle, fumbling with it; frustration making my fingers clumsy. The leather slips, and I growl, "What kind of woman-proof belt is this?"

He chuckles then, low and dark, the sound vibrating against my neck. He swats my hands away, deftly unbuckling it himself. "Patience, *reina.*"

"Screw patience." I yank his shirt over his head, revealing a chest made of hard planes and ink—skulls, dragons, pin-ups, and motorcycle parts across his pecs. I drag my nails over them and down his abs, savoring his hiss.

I push his jeans down his hips, my knuckles brushing the steel heat of him through his boxers. He groans, and I revel in it. "You're such a tease," I huff.

"Tease?" He unzips my jeans and peels them down my thighs and off. The cold garage air hits my legs, but his palms follow, scorching paths up my body. "You're the one who's been bending over the bike in those tight jeans, whispering Spanish curses like a fucking temptress."

I arch into his touch as his fingers slide under my shirt, rough hands skimming my belly. "You don't even know what I was saying."

"Don't care." He nips my shoulder, biting just hard enough to make me gasp. "Sounded dirty. *Felt* dirty."

"Desk," I pant, nodding toward the office at the back. "*Now.*"

He doesn't argue. He kicks away his jeans and in two strides, he lifts me, my legs locking around his waist as he carries me past toolboxes and half-built engines. My back bumps a shelf, sending something clattering to the floor.

"Careful," he mutters, as a stray lug nut rolls out of the way. "Lily's gonna kill us for making a mess. And we are definitely going to make a *mess*."

"Promises, promises," I shoot back, biting his earlobe.

He deposits me onto the metal desk. Papers scatter, a coffee cup topples over as I yank him closer. Moonlight filters through the window, casting shadows over the invoices and spare parts littering the surface.

He growls, biting my collarbone, as his hands roam over my breasts, thumbs teasing my nipples through my bra. "Damn, these tits...I couldn't help but stare at your cleavage—"

I arch into his touch, the lace chafing in the best way. "Like a starving man."

"I was so hard I *ached*." He unhooks my bra, mouth closing over one pebbled peak. I gasp, fingers twisting in his hair as he licks and sucks, pure relentless heat. His free hand slides down between my legs, and he groans. "Fuck, you're soaked."

"Your fault." I rock against his fingers, needing more. "Always teasing. Flirting. *Looking* at me like—"

"Like I want to eat your hot pussy until you come all over my face?" He nips my inner thigh, dragging my panties down. "Guess what, *mi reina?* I do."

His mouth descends on me, tongue laving my clit with slow, torturous skill. I buck, a broken moan tearing loose. His hands grip my hips, pinning me to the desk as he works me with sinful focus. Every stroke of his tongue, every teasing suck, unravels me further.

"Kyle—*Dios*, I'm—"

He hums against me, the vibration shattering what's left of my control.

I come with a cry, back bowing off the desk. He doesn't let up, drawing out the aftershocks until I'm trembling, my thighs shaking.

Before I can catch my breath, he stands, gripping his cock— *thick*, flushed, *perfect*—and meets my gaze. "Still sure?"

I answer by shoving him into the desk chair and straddling his lap. His hands grope my ass as I sink onto him, both of us gasping at the stretch.

"*God*, you feel…" He sucks my nipple into his mouth, hips rolling up to meet mine.

I ride him hard, nails raking his shoulders. "*Say it.*"

"Like heaven." He grips my hips, thrusting deeper. "Like *mine.*"

The possessive snarl undoes me. I clench around him, my second orgasm barreling through me just as he spills inside me with a guttural groan, forehead pressed to my chest.

For a moment, the only sound is our ragged breathing. The chair creaks beneath us, and somewhere outside, crickets chirp in the summer heat. His lips brush the butterfly tattoo on my wrist—the one I got after the divorce, a symbol of starting over.

"Hey." He tilts my chin up, his thumb smudging the tear I didn't realize had fallen. "You okay?"

I nod, my throat tight. "Just...nobody's ever..." *Wanted me like this.*

He kisses me softly, nothing like the feverish clash from before. "I've got you, Ellie. Always."

The words terrify me. Thrill me. I bury my face in his neck, breathing him in.

His hand strokes my back, patient, until my heartbeat slows. "Hungry? I've got Pop-Tarts in the break room."

I snort-laugh, the tension shattering. "Romantic."

"Hey, I'm a classy guy." His hands slide lower. "Also, the thing about us young guys...round two's on the menu if you—"

But it's Ben's face that flickers in my mind—his threat, his lawyer. My legs tighten around Kyle reflexively.

He must feel it for he pulls back, eyes searching mine. "What's wrong?"

"Nothing." I kiss him, pouring everything I have into it. "Just...don't stop."

He stands abruptly, lifting me with him much too easily, and presses me against the office wall. My legs wrap around him as he fills me again, slow and deep.

"Look at me," he demands, and I do, his blue eyes dark, serious. "This isn't a fling. I want you now *and* forever."

I clutch his shoulders, the words slipping out before I can stop them. "*Te quiero.*"

He stills. "What's that mean?"

I'm falling for you. Too fast, too hard. "It means...drive me to your place after this."

He laughs, the sound rich and warm, and picks up the pace of his thrusts. "You lie."

Two more deep pumps and we're both coming again, howling into the night.

Later, as we stagger to his bike, my legs still shaky, he tangles our fingers together. The mountain air is cool, the stars bright and shiny above us.

"You ready?" he asks, handing me a helmet.

I lean into him, the weight of his arm around my shoulders like an anchor. "You bet I am."

CHAPTER 6
KYLE

E llie's nails dig into my back as I carry her into my cabin, her laughter bouncing off the pine walls. "Since when are you this strong?" she gasps.

"Psshhh, I don't need to be strong to lift you." I wink. "But ever since I noticed you eying my biceps, I may have done a few extra curls on the weight bench."

She smirks as I head straight for my bedroom, and drop her onto the bed. Her hair fans out like spilled ink against my gray sheets, her cheeks still flushed from the ride here. The scent of her—vanilla and motor oil and sex—*wrecks me.*

I crawl over her and she tugs my shirt off, her palms skimming my chest. "You're a damn machine," she mutters, her eyes burning like she wants to devour every inch of me.

God, yes.

"Says the woman who came three times in a grease pit." I hook my thumb under the waistband of her jeans, dragging them down. "Round four, baby. Let's make it count."

But when I lean in to kiss her, she cups my face. "Wait. We need to...talk."

My gut twists. *Here it comes.* The part where she says this was a mistake, that I'm too young, that she's not ready. I roll onto my side, pulling her against me. "Spill it," I rasp, anxious.

She chuckles, tracing the skull tattoo on my bicep, avoiding my eyes. "Ben and I...we tried to have kids." Her voice cracks. "Turns out my body's...broken. Doctor said I couldn't. And Ben didn't want to adopt. Said it felt like a 'compromise.'" She scoffs, the sound bitter.

Her confession guts me. I blink, processing this new information. "Okay," I say slowly. "And how do you feel about that?"

She shrugs. "I used to want them, badly. But after the divorce, I just...stopped thinking about it. It hurt too much."

I tilt her chin up, forcing her to meet my gaze. "I want kids, Ellie. Lots of them. I'd adopt 'em all if I could."

"Really?" She sniffles. "You're okay with that?"

My thumb brushes her cheek. "You do know that Ben's a *pendejo*, right?"

She huffs a laugh. "Obviously."

I smile. "Kids aren't about biology. They're about... showing up. Loving hard." I nod toward the framed photo on my nightstand of Juniper and me grinning under a carnival tent, with Delilah in Isaac's arms and Evan on my shoulders. "Family's what you build. Ask Zoe and Troy, a couple here in Deepwood—they adopted Micah, a teenager, last year, and Chelsea and Peter, as babies before that.

Her eyes soften. "You've thought about this."

"Hell yes. And it became a *real* dream the moment I met you." I kiss her palm. "I want it all, Ellie. A lifetime of your delicious food. A house full of chaos. Grandkids who visit just to steal my tools."

She blinks fast, a tear slipping free. "You're serious."

"Dead-ass." I swipe the tear away, grinning. "But first, let's get you that taqueria."

She sits up, excitement replacing the shadows. "I found a place for sale in Helena! It's got plenty of space, even if the price is a little steep."

"Or," I say, rolling her beneath me again. "What do you think about a food truck? Feed this whole damn mountain, *and* Helena. No rent, less risk."

"I never thought..." She stares at me. "Where would I park it?"

"Here, silly," I say.

"You'd let me park a big food truck on your land?"

"Babe, I'd let you park a *tank* here if it made you smile like that."

She arches up to kiss me, all heat and hope. "You're a genius," she murmurs against my lips.

I stretch out over her, pinning her wrists. "I have good ideas sometimes."

She smiles, then says more seriously. "But I still need to sell the bike. I'm not sure what I'll get for it."

"Let *me* buy the bike."

She freezes. "What? No, that money's for—"

"For your dream. I'll pay double." I kiss her nose. "I'll keep it as a trophy. Proof I stole the best woman alive from that douche canoe."

Her laugh lights up the room. "I want to name my food truck, the *Mariposa Taqueria.*"

"Love it." I nuzzle her neck, sucking lightly. "*Now,* what do I have to do to get you to marry me..."

She blinks, suddenly breathless. "Was that...a proposal?"

"A *pre-proposal.* I'll get a ring. Kneel like you deserve." I trail lower, teeth grazing her collarbone. "Right after I make you come so hard you forget how to make *picadillo con papas.*"

"Kyle—"

"Just say yes, Eloísa."

She fists my hair, tugging my mouth to hers. "*Sí, te quiero.*"

I freeze, my heart hammering away. "I looked that up, you know."

She grins, eyes flashing.

"Say it again."

"*Te quiero, idiota.*"

I growl. "I'm gonna learn Spanish just to dirty-talk you properly."

She locks her legs around my hips and smirks. "I don't doubt it."

EPILOGUE - ELLIE
THREE MONTHS LATER

The lunch rush at the *Mariposa Taqueria* is a beautiful kind of chaos. For me, it's what dreams are made of. The scent of sizzling *carne asada* and fresh cilantro swirls in the air as I hand a heaping plate of *al pastor* tacos to Mrs. Martin, the town's resident octogenarian and my most loyal customer.

"Extra guac, just like you asked," I say, grinning as she eyes the toppings like a kid at a candy store.

"You're a saint, my dear," she says, clutching the plate to her chest. "You've got a real gem here. And speaking of gems...say hello to that sexy mechanic of yours for me. You know, if I were fifty years younger, I'd steal him for myself."

I laugh, wiping my hands on my apron. "Back off, Mrs. M. He's *all mine*."

The food truck's window stays busy for another hour, the line stretching toward McCafferty Customs' garage where Kyle's been slammed all morning. Through the crowd, I catch glimpses of him—his bandana-clad head bent over the engine, his laugh carrying over the rumble of engines as he jokes with Zane. My chest tightens, the way it always does when I watch him work.

Who knew grease and sweat could be this sexy?

By two o'clock, the crowd thins, and I'm scraping the last of the *queso fresco* onto a pair of loaded nachos for Remi and Dax, who've been lurking near the picnic tables like vultures. Remi swipes the plate with a grin. "You're a goddess, Ellie. If Kyle ever screws up, you're mine."

Dax snorts, shoveling a chip into his mouth. "Keep dreamin', St. Claire. You couldn't handle her."

"Damn right she couldn't." Kyle's voice rumbles behind me in the truck, his arms sliding around my waist as he nuzzles my neck. His hands are still streaked with oil, his shirt clinging to his chest in that *just-sweaty-enough* way that makes my pulse skip. "How's my favorite chef?"

I lean into him. "Exhausted. Your fan club ate me out of three pounds of chorizo."

"Well, half these folks only come for the view." He gestures to himself, doing a little hip shake, and I roll my eyes.

"Keep flexing, *cariño*, and I'll make you sleep in the garage."

"Joke's on you—I've got a cot in there." He spins me to face him, his grin softening as he smooths a stray curl behind my ear. "Seriously, though. You killed it today. Proud of you."

Warmth blooms in my chest. Three months ago, I'd have panicked at the thought of someone being proud of me. Now? Now I stand taller. "Couldn't have done it without you," I say, and mean it. Every day with this man is a gift.

His thumb brushes my lip, his eyes darkening. "Nah, *reina*. This is *all* you."

A wolf whistle cuts through the moment. We turn to see Juniper strolling over, baby Delilah strapped to her chest and Evan trailing behind, clutching a toy motorcycle. "Get a room, you two," she teases. "Ellie, these *birria* tacos are *stupidly* good. When are you catering my brother's wedding?"

Kyle chokes on his *horchata,* and I elbow him, smirking. "Whenever he works up the nerve to ask."

"Oh, he'll ask," Juniper says, winking. "He's been pacing around our kitchen all week, practicing his speech with a Ring Pop."

"Traitor," Kyle mutters, but he's grinning as Evan tugs on his jeans, demanding a piggy back ride.

The afternoon slips by in a blur of laughter and limes. By sunset, the truck's spotless, the last of the supplies packed away. Kyle leans against the counter, watching me. "Ready for your surprise?"

I freeze, spatula in hand. "Surprise?"

"Yep." He grabs my wrist, tugging me toward the garage. "And before you argue—it's not a puppy."

"You say that like it's a bad thing," I mutter, but let him lead me inside.

The garage is dim, the usual fluorescent lights replaced by strands of twinkling fairy lights. My breath catches. The McCafferty crew and their wives are all here, along with Juniper, Isaac, and a dozen other familiar faces from town.

A banner hangs above the Sportster, its chrome catching the light.

"Will You Marry Us?" it reads, the *Us* crossed out and replaced with *Him* in sloppy spray paint.

I burst out laughing. "Real subtle, guys!"

I feel lighter than I have in years. As I look around the room, I'm struck by the sense of community, of family. Something I never had with Ben.

Dax's wife, Kendra, who's a badass lawyer, helped me put Ben in his place. She contacted his lawyer and confirmed he had no case against me and the bike. She also said if he ever came near me again, we'd sue for harassment. *I love her.*

Remi and Lily have become like sisters to me, and it's encouraged me to reach out to Letty. Especially now that it looks like I could expand my business.

These wonderful people have become my family and I couldn't be more grateful.

Kyle drops to one knee, pulling a ring box from his pocket. The room falls silent, but all I see is him—his eyes bright, his hands steady, that damn bandana slipping over his brow.

"Eloísa Hamilton," he says, voice rough. "You walked into my shop with a broken bike and a broken heart, and you gave me the best damn deal of my life. You're stubborn, and brilliant, and you make a tamale that could bring me back from the dead." The crowd chuckles, but I'm blinking back tears. "You're my best friend. My family. My *everything*. So, what do you say? Let me be your taste-tester for life and marry me?"

The box opens. The ring is simple, a pear-cut diamond nestled in rose gold, flanked by a tiny butterfly.

It's stunning.

"*God*, you're such a dork," I whisper, but I'm already nodding, pulling him up to kiss me. The garage erupts in cheers, Juniper whooping, Remi chanting *"Food truck discount!"* as Kyle spins me, his laughter against my lips.

When he sets me down, Juniper presses a margarita into my hand, her eyes misty. "I knew he'd nail it."

"Barely," Zane grumbles, but he's smiling as he claps Kyle's shoulder.

Later, as the party winds down, Kyle and I sneak out to the overlook on the Sportster, the valley sprawled below us like a painting. The ring winks on my finger, the diamond catching the moonlight.

"You really want this?" I ask quietly, and we lay on the flat rock, fingers entwined. "Forever's an awfully long time."

His thumb brushes my tattoo. "Forever's not long enough, *amor*," he says, his voice low and breathy. "Besides, we've got a food truck to run. Kids to adopt. Maybe a few more bikes to rebuild."

"You're so right." I lean into him, the future stretching ahead, bright and boundless, and full of love.

~

ROUGH RIDE

CHAPTER 1
MASON

The gleaming metal letters of the McCafferty Customs sign almost mock me from the brick facade above. Shouldn't they be tarnished beyond recognition at this point, corroded by bad decisions and false promises like my life?

My throat tightens as I kill the engine of my beaten-up Ford, my last remaining possession after my spectacular Hollywood flameout.

I stare at the garage doors like they might swallow me whole. Christ, I used to strut through them like I owned the place. And now I'm crawling back with my tail between my legs, begging for scraps?

Mason *"The Fuckup"* West. Thirty-nine years old. Broke. Living with his *much-too-kind* parents.

My phone buzzes with my mother's third text in twenty minutes:

> Did you get there yet? Don't be late! Dash is
> expecting you.

I swipe it away, grinding my teeth. Six years ago, I was negotiating TV appearances. Now my mother's reminding me to show up for a job interview like I'm sixteen and applying at a fast-food joint.

Can you blame her, though?

Oh, shut up, self.

The Montana summer is suffocating as I force myself out of the truck. It's hotter than I remember, the humidity weighing thick and oppressive on my shoulders. I can hear the familiar symphony of metal on metal, power tools singing, and classic rock blaring from ancient speakers inside the garage.

This was home once.

Before you decided you were too good for it.

I straighten my spine and push the nagging voice down again as I open the office door. The bell above it jingles, and I'm hit immediately by the smells—oil, grease, metal shavings. I'd forgotten how they permeate everything, become part of your skin, your hair. In Los Angeles, I'd spent a fortune on designer cologne trying to mask the lingering scent that screamed *motorcycle mechanic* that never quite washed away.

"Well, well. The prodigal son returns," Dash McCafferty says, wiping his hands on a clean rag as he approaches the counter.

He's aged since the show...there's more silver in his dark hair, deeper lines around his eyes, but he still has that commanding presence, the quiet confidence of a man who knows exactly who he is. Unlike me.

"Hey, Dash." My voice, surprisingly, comes out steadier than I feel. "Thanks for—"

"Save it." He cuts me off with a dismissive wave. His ice-blue eyes, always so perceptive, sweep over me, taking stock of the remains of the guy who abandoned this place for Hollywood glory. "You look like shit."

I bark out a laugh. "Thanks a bunch. Feel like it too."

"Fame not all it's cracked up to be?" There's no sympathy

in his tone, just a slight hint of satisfaction that makes me want to crawl under a rock.

"Turns out when the cameras stop rolling, so does the money." I force a smirk. "Who knew?"

"*Everyone,*" a female voice cuts in, sharp as a freshly honed blade. "Everyone but you, dumbass."

I turn, and my breath catches.

Holy hell.

She's leaning against the doorframe—tall, lithe, arms crossed—clearly saying "don't fuck with me." Tattoos snake up her arms like living art: gears, flames, and raven wings disappear under a tank top that hugs her curves in all the right places. Her jet-black hair with neon green streaks is pulled back in a messy ponytail, framing a face that makes my heart stutter. Full lips painted blood red, sharp cheekbones, and hazel eyes flecked with burnt gold have me in a chokehold. And said eyes are currently narrowed on me with a look of pure disgust.

Somehow, it only makes her more attractive.

Remi St. Claire, the shop's goth goddess mechanic. I recognize her from her social media posts on Insta, but they don't do her justice. Not by a mile.

"I guess so," I manage, offering my hand. "Mason West. You must be Remi."

She stares at my outstretched palm dubiously, like I'm offering her a dead rat. "I know who you are," she says, not budging an inch. "Saw your whole meltdown on Season 2. Nice tantrum over the paint job. Super professional."

Heat crawls up my neck. *That fucking episode.* The producers edited it to make me look like a prima donna, throwing a fit because a client changed specifications last minute. I'd actually been frustrated about safety concerns, but that doesn't make for juicy reality TV.

"You know what those shows are like," I say with forced lightness. "All scripted drama."

"Bullshit." Her eyes flash with a spark of green fire that zips straight to my groin. "I know a sellout when I see one."

"Remi..." Dash warns, but there's no real heat in it. He turns to me. "Look, I'll be straight with you, Mason. You're only getting this chance because you were a damn good mechanic and designer before your head got too big, and we're slammed with work right now. But things have changed around here. We run a tight ship these days."

I nod. "I understand."

"I hope you do." Dash raises an eyebrow. "You're starting at the bottom. And since I don't have time to babysit, Remi here's going to be your supervisor."

"What?" I can't hide my shock. She looks at least ten years younger than me.

Remi's smile is all teeth and no warmth, like a shark's. "Problem with that, Reality Boy?"

"N-no," I say quickly. Too quickly. "No problem at all."

"Good." Dash rubs his hands together. "Then let's get you oriented. Zane's out on a bank run with Lily right now, and Kyle's busy repairing his wife's food truck this morning. But you'll meet them soon. For now, Remi will show you around."

"I know my way around...?" I protest weakly.

"Hmph. Places change," Dash says. "People too...supposedly." The way he eyes me makes it clear he's reserving judgment on that last part.

He heads to his office, leaving me alone with Remi, who's studying me with the kind of scrutiny usually reserved for particularly disgusting insects.

"So," I say, desperate to break the ice. "Where do we start?"

"You can organize the parts closet," she says, jerking her thumb toward the back. "Kyle tore it apart last week looking for something he swore he left there." She rolls her eyes. "Fucking idiot turned the place into a disaster zone. I'm surprised Lily didn't kill him."

I blink at her. I used to design custom choppers worth tens of thousands for the rich and famous, for fuck's sake. "Seriously?"

"What, the big TV star's too good for grunt work now?" She cocks her head, the movement sending her green-streaked ponytail flipping over her shoulder. "Too important to organize nuts and bolts? Look, buddy, you want back in, prove you actually give a shit about the craft and this shop, not just the spotlight."

Ouch. Her words hit hard. Because she's right, that's exactly what happened. I got so caught up in being "Mason West: Motorcycle Master" that I forgot why I fell in love with building bikes in the first place.

"Okay," I say, rolling up my sleeves. "Parts closet it is."

She smirks, glancing down at my arms for a split second before snapping her eyes back to mine. "It'll be a miracle if you last the week."

As she walks away, I catch myself watching the jiggle of her sweet ass in her black Dickie's and admiring the confident set of her shoulders. The woman is fire and steel covered in tattoo ink and dripping with attitude, and she has a clear hatred of me.

So why is she making me *ache* in a way I never have before?

I march over to the parts closet, determined to organize the hell out of it. If this is what it takes to rebuild my life—to reclaim my dignity and prove I'm more than just another washed-up celebrity—then I'll give it everything I've got.

Because honestly, I've got nowhere else to go. And despite Remi's prediction, I'm *not* walking away this time.

CHAPTER 2
REMI

I stomp into the garage in a sour mood, kicking the metal dust off my Docs with even more fervor than usual. Just the sight of him—Mason West, washed-up reality star, *supposed* motorcycle master—makes my skin prickle with irritation. Yes, *irritation*. He's been here three days, and I've been watching him like a hawk circling wounded prey.

He's currently bent over a shelf, clipboard in hand, finishing up with the parts closet he's been fixing up in the wake of Kyle's tantrum last week. He's actually done a decent job, but I'll eat a timing belt before I'll tell him that.

"Mornin'," he says, looking up at me. Fine lines fan out from his deep navy eyes, evidence of his thirty-nine years, though you wouldn't guess it from looking at the rest of him. His beefy arms flex as he lifts a carburetor onto another shelf, heat pooling low in my belly before I force myself to look away.

"We got a job, meathead," I say, tossing him a clean rag. "Forget the closet for now."

He catches the rag one-handed, with the practiced grace of

someone who's spent a lifetime in places like this. "What's the job?"

"Some emergency," I grumble, already walking toward the bay doors where Zane and Kyle are unloading a mangled Ducati from a flatbed. "Rich tourist crashed his bike up on Eagle Summit Pass. Needs it fixed yesterday."

Mason follows me, his heavy boots loud on the concrete. "What happened to it?"

"Idiot took a curve too fast, crashed into the guardrail." I tap the twisted frame. "The owner walked away, but the bike wasn't so lucky."

"Shit," he whistles. When he crouches down to assess the damage, his jeans strain to accommodate his...bulk. His thick fingers trace the bent fork with a gentleness that inexplicably makes my insides clench.

"Another rich asshole who thinks money can buy skill," Dax grunts, appearing from under a nearby lift. "No respect for the machine."

"Or the mountain," Zane adds dryly. "Cops found pieces two hundred feet down the slope."

Kyle snickers, spinning a wrench between his fingers. "Ten bucks says he was showing off for a chick."

"And twenty says she dumped him right after he crashed!" I shoot back. Kyle's laugh echoes through the garage.

"Zane, where's Lily today?" I ask, as Dash emerges from the office, tapping on his tablet. Typically, she'd be the one handing out the workload directives.

"Just a quick doc appointment," he answers.

"Oh." She didn't mention it to me. Then again, I've been up to my ass trying to keep my wits about me with Mason.

Dash clears his throat and taps the tablet again. "Client's offering triple our normal rate if we can get it done by Friday. He's flying back to Chicago then."

"*Friday?*" Kyle yelps. "That's three days from now. This is at least a week-long job."

Dash shrugs. "Guess we'd better find someone who can work miracles, then." His eyes slide to Mason, then me. "Remi, you and Mason take the lead on this one okay?"

"What?!" The word explodes out of me. "Why not put Kyle on it? Or Dax?"

"Dax is finishing the Thompson build, and Kyle's got that vintage Indian to restore," Dash says calmly, raising an eyebrow. "What? You don't think you can handle it?"

I bristle. "I can handle anything."

"Good." He nods toward Mason. "Because this guy knows Ducatis better than anyone else here."

I *hate* that Dash is right...but he is. Mason specialized in European bikes on the show, customizing them for celebrities with more money than taste.

"Fine," I mumble, grabbing the closest toolbox. "Let's get this disaster on the lift."

For the next few hours, Mason and I work in relative silence, broken only by sporadic requests for tools and occasional grunts of frustration. Annoyingly, the guy clearly knows what he's doing. His hands move with quiet, confident skill, diagnosing problems and finding solutions. It's like the bike is speaking directly to his fingertips.

When he stretches to reach a spot, his shirt rides up, revealing a toned stomach and a trail of dark hair disappearing into the waistband of his jeans. My mouth waters, and I nearly drop the socket wrench I'm holding.

"Fuck! This fork's completely shot," I say, struggling with a bent piece of metal, desperate to take my mind off the relentless heat spreading through me.

"Hang on." Mason slides in beside me, his shoulder

brushing mine. Electricity immediately zings down my spine. "Let me try something."

He pulls a specialized tool from his personal kit—one I haven't seen before—and applies pressure at exactly the right angle. The metal groans, then yields, actually straightening enough to be salvageable.

"Where'd you learn that trick?" I ask, unable to keep the admiration from my voice.

He smiles. "Guy in Barcelona. He had a shop that specialized in crash recoveries." He pauses, then adds quietly, "It was when I was traveling. Before the show."

I study him, noticing the genuine care in his movements. It's not the performative showmanship I remember from TV, but the authentic reverence of someone who respects the machine under his hands. When he pokes out his tongue in concentration, more awkward heat sears through me.

"Huh…" is all I can manage.

By late afternoon, we've made surprising progress. The twisted frame has been salvaged, and we've sourced replacement parts for what can't be repaired. It's still a huge job, but suddenly Friday doesn't seem impossible.

I stretch, cracking my back after hours hunched over the bike. When I turn, I catch Mason watching me, his gaze darkening as it travels over my body. My nipples tighten under my tank top, and he quickly looks away, his focus returning to the fuel line he's flushing.

Fuck.

"We should break for lunch," I say, wiping my hands on my pants. "Can't rebuild a Ducati on an empty stomach."

A smile spreads across his face, transforming his features from merely handsome to something that makes my core throb with need. "Lead the way."

In the break room, Kyle's already demolished half a pizza, and Dax is nursing a protein shake that looks like liquid dirt.

"How's the disaster bike?" Kyle asks around a mouthful of pepperoni.

"Better than expected," I admit, dropping into a chair and stealing a slice from his box. "Reality Boy actually knows his stuff."

"Hey! Get your own pizza, gremlin," Kyle protests, yanking the box away.

"Ellie says you need to learn to share," I laugh, snatching another slice. I don't know how the dumbass managed to snag such a perfect wife, who for bonus points makes the best Mexican food I've ever had.

"Yeah, yeah," Kyle agrees. "But *she* makes it worth my while when I share. *You guys* are just assholes."

Dax and I fist bump across the table. "Aww, maybe Dax'll slip you some tongue, if you ask nicely."

"Ew," Kyle grumbles, shuddering.

"Double ew," Dax grunts.

Mason raises an eyebrow as I slide him a slice of pizza on a paper plate. "You guys still order from Pizza Palace, I see."

"Yup. *Some* things never change," Dash says, entering with a stack of invoices. He tosses them on the table before grabbing a slice.

The pointed remark hangs in the air. Mason's shoulders tense, but he doesn't comment.

Dash's expression softens slightly. "I need to talk to you guys." He glances between Mason and me. "The Mountain West Bike Expo is next weekend in Boulder. We've got a premier booth this year, and I need our best on-site."

My pizza slice freezes halfway to my mouth. "You're sending us to Boulder?"

"The shop needs to send someone, and you two understand both the technical and aesthetic aspects." Dash folds his arms. "Plus, I've watched the way you work together. You make a good team."

"I can do the show myself," I protest.

"No. Mason's got more experience handling these events. Meanwhile, you've got the design eye we need," Dash counters. "It's about showcasing what McCafferty Customs can do."

I turn to Mason, expecting a smug smile. Instead, he looks as uncomfortable as I feel.

"How long?" he asks Dash.

"Four days. Leave Thursday morning, back Sunday night."

Four days. With Mason. *Alone.* My gut churns at the thought, even as another traitorous part of me imagines him in a hotel room, bare-chested, fresh from a shower, with water droplets trailing down his massive pecs—

"Do we have a choice?" I ask, already knowing the answer.

Dash smiles mildly. "Not if you want that raise we talked about."

Shit. I've been angling hard for that raise for a while now.

"Fine," I concede, stabbing at my pizza like it personally offended me. "But I get to drive the trailer."

"No problem," Dash agrees. "I'll make the arrangements."

As Dash walks away, Mason catches my eye. "For the record, I'm not thrilled about this either."

"Why?" I challenge. "Afraid being seen with a common grease monkey like me will do more damage to your TV star image?"

He surprises me by letting out a spontaneous laugh that lacks the polish of his camera-ready chuckle. "Pretty sure that image is beyond salvaging." He hesitates. "I've seen your work, Remi. You're incredible at what you do. I'd be an idiot not to *at least try* to learn something from you."

The compliment catches me off guard, sending a warm flutter first through my chest, then decidedly lower. I shift in my seat, uncomfortably aware of the throb between my legs.

"Save the charm for Boulder," I mutter, standing abruptly. "We've got a bike to fix."

I trudge back to the Ducati, more annoyed at myself than at him. I'm starting to wonder if there might be more to this guy than the fame-hungry sellout I've spent years despising.

And that's a complication I absolutely do not need.

CHAPTER 3
MASON

The following Thursday, we're three hours into the twelve-hour drive to Boulder, Remi skillfully maneuvering the trailer carrying our showcase bikes along the Montana highway. I've already realized she likes being in control—the wheel in her hands, everything on her terms. Not that I mind. In fact, something about a woman who takes charge like Remi does has my cock thickening in a way I wasn't prepared for.

So far, our conversation has consisted of monosyllabic grunts, debating the timing of the next rest stop and whether the radio should stay on classic rock or switch to her personal playlist. Needless to say, that's a bunch of goth bands I've never heard of wailing about existential despair.

I've been stealing glances at her when I think she's not looking—her fingers tapping the steering column in perfect rhythm, her jaw clenching when we pass a particularly shitty driver, the neon green in her hair catching the sunlight through the windshield.

"Take a picture, it'll last longer," she says without once looking away from the road, her voice razor-sharp.

Busted.

"Sorry," I mutter, shifting in my seat. "Just trying to figure you out."

"There's nothing *to* figure out. What you see is what you get." She flexes her tattooed fingers and my eyes are drawn to the shiny black manicure she had done just for this weekend. *Coffin nails*, she'd called them. I wonder how they'd feel raking down my back.

I snort. "And what's that? A tough-as-nails goth chick who hates my guts based on a reality show that was edited to hell and back? You *know* that's what they do."

Her eyes flicker to me briefly, then return to the road. "Please. Nobody held a gun to your head to be on that show. You wanted the fame. The money. The recognition."

"Maybe," I admit, watching the mountain pines blur past. "But maybe there were other reasons too, at least at first."

That gets her attention. "Like what?"

I hesitate, weighing how much to tell her. My fingers pick at a loose thread on my jeans. "My dad got sick right before the show started taping. Parkinson's. His medical bills were piling up. Frankly, the TV offer came at exactly the right time."

Remi's silent for a long moment, absorbing this. "Okayyyy… But you didn't have to become such a raging dick about it."

I laugh loudly. "No, you're right, I didn't. That part's on me." I turn to look out the window, remembering the sudden rush of attention, how quickly it went to my head and warped my priorities. "It's weird, you get a taste of that spotlight, and suddenly everyone's telling you how special you are. How you deserve better than some small-town garage. It's…intoxicating."

"B'aww, poor widdle celebrity," she mocks, but there's less fire in it now.

I shake my head. "I'm not asking for sympathy, Remi. Just setting the record straight."

She raises an eyebrow, the silver piercing through it winking in the light. "So... What happened in L.A.? The show made it look like you were set for life."

The question scrapes painfully against memories I've tried to bury. The failed custom shop catering to celebrities who ghosted me when the next big thing came along. The over-priced home I could no longer afford. The desperate pitches for more TV projects that went nowhere.

"I guess I believed my own hype," I admit quietly. "Opened a high-end shop with money I didn't have, thinking my 'star power' would bring in A-list clients. I mean, women... and men...threw themselves at me, wanting to be seen with 'that motorcycle guy from TV.' But when the money ran out, they vanished." I rub a hand over my face tiredly. "Six months in, I was drowning in debt. A year later, I had to sell everything I owned to cover the mortgage, including most of my tools. I still couldn't stop the foreclosure."

I sigh and stare at the highway stretching endlessly ahead. "Now I feel like a ghost haunting his own life."

"Jesus," she mutters. "That's dark. Even for me."

"Yeah. My fifteen minutes were up, and I had nothing to show for it except bankruptcy and my parents' guest bedroom." My smile probably looks more like a grimace. "Not exactly the triumphant return I'd pictured."

The highway stretches before us endlessly as Remi digests this. She chews her bottom lip, and I try not to stare at the way the dark red lipstick makes her mouth look so damn kissable.

"What about you?" I ask, desperate to shift the focus of the conversation. "How'd you end up at McCafferty's?"

She lifts a shoulder. "My dad owned a small auto shop in Bozeman, so I grew up learning the trade. When his business went under, nobody would hire a female mechanic." Her knuckles whiten on the wheel. "The first three shops told me to apply for the receptionist position instead. The fourth said I'd look better in a bikini washing cars."

Anger boils beneath my skin. "Fucking assholes."

"Yeah. Dash was the only one who had me rip apart an engine to prove myself." A small smile plays over her lips. "When I reassembled it in half the time his best guy could, he hired me on the spot."

"Smart man."

She glances at me. "Honestly, that's why it pissed me off so much when you left. You had what every mechanic dreams of —a shop that valued skill over bullshit—and you threw it all away for cameras and groupies."

"I know," I say softly. "Believe me, I know."

We lapse into silence again, but it's different now, less hostile, more contemplative. Almost comfortable, but not quite. The miles tick by, and the Montana landscape gives way to Wyoming.

We make a quick stop at a roadside diner for lunch, the neon OPEN sign flickering like a distress beacon. After we eat, we're back in the cab of the truck. Even with regular bathroom breaks and another stop for dinner, by the time we pull into the Boulder hotel parking lot it's late, my back is screaming, and my legs have gone numb.

Remi seems pretty stiff, too, rolling her shoulders as we climb out of the truck.

"I'll check us in," she says, grabbing her purse from the backseat.

I nod, stretching my arms overhead until my spine gives a satisfying crack. When she returns, her expression is murderous.

"There's been a 'slight booking error'," she says, the air

quotes practically visible. "They have us in the same room, and it's the last one they have."

My stomach twists into a complicated knot. "Twin beds?" I ask hopefully.

"Guess again." She tosses a keycard at me. "One king bed. Apparently, there's multiple conferences happening in town this weekend and everything's booked solid."

"I'll sleep on the floor," I offer immediately.

She rolls her eyes. "With that old man back? Please. You'll be whining all night."

"I'm not *that* old," I protest, hefting both our duffel bags despite her attempts to grab hers. "Besides, it's pretty obvious you'd rather sleep in a den of rattlesnakes than share a bed with me."

"You're not wrong," she says. "But we're adults. We can share a bed without making it weird." She stalks toward our room. "Just stay on your side and keep your hands to yourself. Otherwise, I break your fingers."

I follow her, swallowing hard. I'm not worried about my hands—I'm worried about the part in my pants that seems to have a mind of its own whenever she's around. She'd probably break that, too.

The room is decent enough...clean, if generic, the bathroom bigger than I expected. The bed itself dominates the space, looking both impossibly large and terrifyingly small at the same time.

"Dibs on the right side," Remi announces, tossing her leather jacket on a chair.

"Fine by me." I set our bags down, suddenly intensely conscious of how small the space feels.

She reaches for her duffel. "I'm gonna shower. Been marinating in those truck fumes all day."

"Sounds good. I'll check on the bikes."

She disappears into the bathroom, and I exhale slowly, sinking onto the edge of the bed, my head in my hands.

This is hell. Beautiful, impossible hell.

Four days. Working together, eating together, and sleeping mere inches apart Can I make it?

When I hear the shower turn on, I escape to the parking lot, needing both fresh air and distance from the idea of Remi naked on the other side of the door, water cascading over her sexy, tattooed body.

I'm so incredibly fucked.

The cool evening air helps clear my head as I check the trailer locks and inspect the shop's showcase bikes. By the time I return, Remi's already propped up in bed, her damp hair fanned out on the pillow, scrolling on her phone.

Type O Negative, her T-shirt says. I guess that's a band and not her blood type. The loose neckline exposes one sexy shoulder. Christ, I'm dying to kiss the stark white skin between the ink.

I casually toss a few snacks that I bought from the vending machine onto her nightstand. "In case you get hungry."

"Thanks. Bikes okay?" she asks, not looking up.

"All good." I grab my wash bag and retreat to the bathroom.

The cold shower does little to temper the heat coursing through me. When I emerge in my gym shorts and a worn T-shirt, the overhead light is off, just a bedside lamp illuminating Remi's side of the room.

"Don't hog the blankets," she warns as I slip under the covers, maintaining maximum distance between us.

"Wouldn't dream of it, ma'am."

She clicks off the lamp, plunging us into darkness. I can still sense her presence—the subtle dip of the mattress, the crisp scent of her hair, the warmth radiating across no-man's-land between us.

"Remi?" I whisper.

"Yeah?" she mumbles, already sounding half-asleep.

"Thanks for listening today. I know it's hard when you... you know...hate me."

She's quiet so long I think she's fallen asleep. Then: "I don't hate you, Mason. I just don't trust you. Yet."

The "yet" hangs there in the dark, a faint, fragile possibility that makes my heart beat a little faster.

CHAPTER 4
REMI

I didn't sleep for shit last night.

How could I? Mason's massive body was radiating heat like a furnace on the other side of the bed. His breathing eventually evened out, meanwhile I just lay there, staring at the ceiling, conscious of every shift of the mattress, every rustle of the sheets. I kept telling myself it was just the physical proximity putting me on edge, not the way he'd laid himself bare about what he'd been through when we were in the truck.

Not the way his husky voice sounded so damn broken when he'd straight up said I hated him.

My response, surprisingly, sounded like a promise. One I'm not sure I can keep.

Morning doesn't improve things. I find myself curled toward him, my face inches away from his broad, tattooed chest. His arm is stretched across the pillow above my head, fingers slightly tangled in my hair. For a moment, I imagine waking up under very different circumstances—after a night of him exploring every inch of my body, learning what makes me gasp and writhe, and making me totally come apart beneath those rough hands.

I jerk away, the movement startling him awake.

"Wha—?" He blinks sleepily, confused. It's so fucking cute I legit want to punch something.

"Up and at 'em, TV Boy," I say gruffly. "We've got a bike expo to dominate."

He rubs his eyes, hair sticking up in tufts. "What time is it?"

"Seven. Setup's in an hour." I slip out of bed, making sure my T-shirt covers my butt. "I call first shower."

I don't wait for an answer, just grab my clothes and escape to the bathroom. There. Now I can breathe without inhaling his heady scent of sleep and man-musk that does dangerous things to my insides.

We arrive at the show venue, a massive convention center that's all gleaming glass and industrial metal. Our booth occupies some prime real estate directly across from the main entrance. Dash wasn't exaggerating when he said he'd got us a primo spot.

"Damn," Mason whistles low. "Dash went all out."

I nod, unpacking the custom backdrop Lily designed. It's got the McCafferty logo—a snarling wolf's head in gleaming chrome—and stunning photos of our best builds. "Dash has been strategic about maintaining the shop's reputation and positive buzz from the TV show while still downplaying a lot of the negative fallout. He's got great business sense there."

The subtle dig slips out automatically, and Mason flinches.

"Look, I know I fucked up," he says quietly, setting up the lighting around our showcase bike, a sleek café racer that I designed myself with matte black detailing and bronze accents. "But I'm trying to make it right, okay?"

Something in his tone makes me glance over. He's not looking at me, he's focused instead on adjusting the display, but there's a vulnerability in the set of his shoulders that I'm not used to.

"The lighting looks good," I offer, a small olive branch.

His smile lights up his entire face, and my stomach flip-flops. "And your bike design is incredible. Balancing modern elements and the vintage frame? Pure genius. Totally sick."

Heat crawls up my neck at the compliment. "Pfft, it's just math and aesthetics."

"Fuck no. It's *art*." His gaze is intense, like he can see straight through me. "You're an artist, Remi. Own it."

Before I can come up with a response that doesn't involve kissing that smug mouth, a voice interrupts us.

"Well, well. Mason fucking West."

We turn to see a guy with a scraggly dyed black beard and a beer gut straining against a hideous leather vest approaching our booth. His nose is red, probably from years of drinking, and his smile is more sleaze than anything else.

"Sid." Mason's tone is neutral but his body tenses. "Didn't know you'd be here."

"And miss my chance to see the fallen star in person? No fucking way," Sid sneers, eyes sliding over to me. "Who's this? A groupie? Or they hiring centerfolds to play mechanics these days?"

Every muscle in my body tenses up. "I'm Remi St. Claire, designer at McCafferty Customs. Who the hell are you?"

"Sid Henderson. I run Highway Hellcats out of Denver." He eyes me up and down like I'm a cut of meat in a butcher's display case. "Pretty thing like you could do better than playing second fiddle to this old washed-up has-been."

Mason steps forward, a muscle ticking in his jaw. "She's not playing second fiddle to anyone. Remi's more talented than you, me, or any other mechanic I've ever worked with."

"Sure, sure." Sid leans closer to me. "When you get tired of slumming it with reality trash, come see me. I'll show you how a real man runs a shop."

Don't hit him, Remi. Keep it professional.

"Thanks, but I already work with real men. *And* women. All of us could design circles around whatever overpriced, mid-life crisis toys you're peddling."

Sid's face darkens. "You little bi—"

"*Watch it*, asshole." Mason steps between us, his voice deceptively calm but his body coiled tight like a spring.

Sid backs up, smirking. "Not worth it. See ya round, losers."

As he saunters away, I suppress the urge to throw something heavy at his head. "What a fucking piece of work."

"Sorry about that." Mason runs a hand through his hair. "The man's a Class A jerk. I use him as an example of who I *don't* want to become."

I smile. "Good call."

"Not always a meathead," he says with a smile, tapping his temple.

"You didn't have to defend me," I point out.

He meets my gaze, something fierce and protective in his eyes. "Sure I did. That miserable prick has no right to treat you like that."

Ugh. Why does he have to be so damn kind?

My panties get noticeably damp as the moment stretches between us.

Finally, he clears his throat and turns back to the display. "Let's finish setting up before any more assholes show up."

The rest of the day passes in a blur: bike enthusiasts, industry insiders, potential clients. Mason handles them with an easy confidence that never veers into the arrogance I'd secretly been worried about. He directs technical questions to me without hesitation, highlighting my contributions to each build with genuine respect.

I find myself watching him when he's not looking, noticing the way his face lights up when describing our process or how his hands move as he explains the custom fabrication, and the patience he shows even with the most clueless questions.

This isn't the preening TV personality I remember. This is a man who genuinely loves motorcycles, and the craft of building them.

Others notice, too, and at one point, Mason's surrounded by a gaggle of giggling women—all glossy lips and hungry eyes. *So gross.*

"Maybe you and I could grab a drink later," one of them purrs.

His smile is polite but distant. "No thanks. I'm here to work."

Is it wrong that I *love* the confused expression that spreads across her stupid face?

When the women finally disperse, I toss Mason a water bottle. "Playboy Mason turning down busty admirers? Color me shocked!"

He unscrews the cap, his thick throat working as he drinks. "Not interested in fans. I prefer women who know how to get their hands dirty." His gaze lingers on my mouth, and I look away.

Shit. The AC *must* be broken.

By late afternoon, we've collected a stack of business cards from serious prospective clients and several invitations to collaborate with other shops. One magazine editor wants to feature our café racer in next month's issue.

"We make a good team," Mason says as we lock up the booth for the night. "Admit it."

I roll my eyes but can't suppress a small smile. "We...don't suck. How's that?"

He laughs, the sound warm and genuine. "Holy high praise from Remi St. Claire! I'll take it."

We grab some quick tacos from a food truck outside... which, for the record, are not *nearly* as good as Ellie's...then head back to the hotel room. The easy camaraderie of the day evaporates, replaced, at least for me, by the acute awareness of sharing such a small, intimate space.

I grab my sleep shirt and retreat into the bathroom, trying to ignore the flutter in my stomach as I pass him. When I emerge again, he's sitting on the edge of the bed, phone in hand, frowning at the screen.

"Everything okay?" I ask, settling on my side of the bed.

He hesitates, then turns the phone toward me. It's an email from "Mark Stevens, Producer" with the subject line: COME-BACK OPPORTUNITY.

"They want me back," he says quietly. "Some new motor-cycle competition show. Celebrity judges, big prize money, the whole bit."

My heart sinks. Man, the universe has a sick sense of humor.

"You going to take it?" I keep my voice carefully neutral, sitting next to him on the bed.

"Dunno." He sets the phone down and gazes into the middle distance. "A year ago, I would have jumped at it." His eyes move to mine, dark and searching. "Now I'm not sure fame is what I want anymore."

Something in the tension that's been building inside me since that first day in the garage cracks open.

"What do you want, Mason?" The question comes out quiet and breathy.

He leans closer, the mattress dipping under his weight. "Something honest. Something real."

My hand lifts of its own accord, my fingers trembling as they trace the stubble along his jaw. He inhales quickly, eyes widening with surprise when my thumb grazes his full lower lip.

"Remi?" he breathes, my name a question.

I don't answer with words. Instead, I press my mouth to his. For one heart-stopping moment, he's frozen in shock. Then he groans deeply, his hand sliding into my hair as he kisses me back.

...And everything explodes.

CHAPTER 5
MASON

Remi's mouth plunders mine demandingly, tasting like the lemon-lime soda she had at dinner. My brain short-circuits as her hands fist my shirt, pulling me closer with a hunger that matches my own.

I've thought about this moment more times than I'd care to admit—in the shop whenever she bends over an engine, during our shared silences in the truck, last night when her luscious body was inches away. But nothing compares to the reality of Remi's lips moving against mine and her tongue sweeping into my mouth with such fervor.

I groan, sliding my palm up to cup her jaw, my thumb stroking her high cheekbone. She tastes like rebellion and salvation rolled into one. I'm drowning in her, and god help me, I never want to come up for air.

When she leans into me, her weight pushing me back toward the mattress, something wild unfurls in my chest. I slide my hands down to her waist, gripping the soft cotton of her T-shirt, desperate to touch her skin underneath.

She tears away, panting hard, palms slamming against me. Her hazel eyes go wide with something like panic.

"I can't—" she gasps, pushing back, putting space between us, shaking her head. "This isn't right."

The rejection hits me like a bucket of ice water. "Remi..."

She stands, running a shaky hand through her hair, tangling the green streaks I've become obsessed with. "This makes a mess of everything. We work together. You're probably going back to TV. I'm not interested in being some quick pit stop until the next shiny thing comes along."

I rise to my feet, need clawing at my insides. "Is that what you think this is?"

"I think some producer will dangle a camera in your face and you'll vanish. Just like you did before." She crosses her arms over her chest, uncertainty in her eyes.

I take a tentative step toward her, then another when she doesn't back away. "Remi, I've wanted you since the moment I saw you standing in that doorway, looking at me like I was something you'd scraped off your boot. Nobody's ever called me on my shit the way you do."

Her lips twitch, almost smiling. "Yeah, well, someone should have done it sooner."

I shake my head, frustrated. "I'm not that guy anymore. I'm not gonna leave at the drop of a hat for a slim chance at fame."

"Prove it." Her eyes flash, challenge and fear warring in that green-gold gaze. "*Prove* you want this—want *me*—more than your fucking ego."

"Tell me what I need to do," I say. "You want me to beg?" My voice drops, rough with need as I sink to my knees on the floor in front of her. "Or lick your boots? I'll do it. *Nothing* is off the table with you, Remi."

Her breath hitches. For a heartbeat, she stares down at me, her perfect lips parted.

I look up at her from this new vantage point. Christ, she's

magnificent, suddenly all fierce confidence and barely contained power.

She lifts a socked foot and plants it on my chest, gently pushing me until I'm sitting back on my heels.

"Worship my feet," she says, her eyes never leaving mine.

The command liquefies my spine.

I swallow hard, reaching for her.

"No hands," she warns.

A shiver wracks my body at her tone as I place my hands behind my head, lacing my fingers. I'm not used to surrendering control like this. But with Remi, just knowing that it pleases her turns me on more than I ever have been in my life.

I tug off her sock—a mid-calf thing, black with little skull patterns—with my teeth. Her bare foot is pale and delicate, the toes painted a dark red.

I look up and find her watching me with such raw hunger that my cock throbs painfully against the zipper of my jeans.

I lower my mouth to her foot, pressing my lips to her soft skin, the contact sending electricity sparking through my veins. She moans as I drag my tongue along the high arch, licking and kissing, sucking each of her toes.

"*Fuck*," she breathes, fists clenched at her sides, removing her right foot from my chest and replacing it with the left. "Now, the other one."

I repeat the process, taking my time, savoring her little gasps and the way her thighs tremble. When I'm done, I rest my cheek against her ankle, waiting for what comes next.

"Stand up," she orders. I do so, my legs stiff from kneeling.

Her hands make quick work of my belt, then my jeans, shoving them down to my ankles along with my boxers. My cock springs free, rock-hard and aching for her touch.

"Onto the bed," she commands, pushing me back. "Arms up and out."

I obey, my breath coming in quick bursts. She moves over to the side of the bed where we dropped the bag of trailer gear. She reaches down and pulls out some heavy-duty bike restraints—thick nylon cuffs used to secure the motorcycles.

"Now they're for restraining *you*," she explains, seeing my confusion.

"Very resourceful," I manage, my voice strangled as she wraps them around my wrists, anchoring me to the bed.

When she straddles me, I'm in heaven—the weight of her and the bite of the straps *delicious*.

"Let me know if it gets too much for your shoulders," she says, suddenly concerned.

"All systems go," I rush to assure her.

She smirks, her confidence returning as she trails her fingers down my chest, nails scraping over my nipples.

Fuck. Me.

"And if not?" she whispers, right in my ear.

"I'll say 'red.' Meaning stop."

"*Good boy*," she murmurs. Those two words go straight to my cock, nearly making me come right then and there.

She takes her time exploring my body, touching, teasing, kissing the contours of my chest and the ridges of my stomach, finding the sensitive spots that make me arch and curse. When she finally wraps her hand around my aching cock, I practically levitate off the bed.

"Look at you," she whispers, her voice thick as she strokes me with excruciating slowness. "So hard for me already. Your cock is practically begging for release, isn't it."

My hips buck involuntarily, desperate for more friction. "Please," I groan, the muscles in my thighs tensing.

"Please...what?" She tightens her grip just enough to make me gasp, her thumbnail sliding over the sensitive head where precum has pooled. "Tell me, Mason."

"I need more," I pant, pulling on the restraints.

"Like *this*?" She speeds up slightly, twisting her hand at the tip. It sends sparks shooting up through the backs of my thighs. My back arches off the bed, a string of curses falling from my lips as insane pressure builds at the base of my cock.

"*That's* it," she encourages, watching me intently. "You're getting close, aren't you. Such a filthy boy. I can feel your cock throbbing in my hand."

I nod frantically, beyond words, teetering right on the edge of release—when suddenly her hand is gone. The abrupt loss of contact leaves me gasping, my cock twitching desperately in the cool air.

"Remi, please," I choke, my voice hoarse with need.

"Not yet," she says, trailing her nails lightly up my inner thigh, making the muscles jump beneath her touch. "I'm enjoying watching you too much. The way your abs tighten, the way your face flushes..." She leans down to whisper in my ear again.

"*The way your cock gets even harder when I tell you no.*"

She wraps her hand around me again, and I'm shocked at how sensitive I've become. Every nerve ending is on fire, my skin slick with sweat as she builds me up again, higher this time, working me into a frenzy.

"You're leaking everywhere," she observes, spreading the moisture around the swollen head with her thumb as my body jerks. "So responsive. So needy."

"Needy for you," I rasp between ragged breaths. "Please, Remi... I'm so close."

"Yes, I can see that," she remarks, increasing her pace until my vision starts to blur at the edges, release agonizingly close, only to stop again, leaving me trembling and incoherent with frustration.

"Jesus *fucking* Christ," I growl, yanking on the restraints.

My cock is an angry purple, so engorged it's almost too much, my heartbeat pulsing along the shaft.

Remi laughs lightly, clearly enjoying her power over me. "Look at your poor cock. So swollen and desperate. I bet you'd come if I just *breathed* on it right now."

To test her theory, she leans down and blows a cool stream of air across the sensitive tip, and I nearly sob at the intense sensation.

"I knew it," she says. "Your whole body is primed, just waiting for permission." Her wicked hand returns to me. "Your pulse is racing. Your thighs are shaking."

Every muscle in my body is as taut as a bowstring, pulled tight with need. When her free hand cups my balls, massaging them gently, I know I won't last much longer.

"Please," I beg, far past caring how pathetic I sound. "I need to come. Remi, I'll do anything."

"*Anything*?" she murmurs, leaning down to brush her lips against mine.

"Fucking anything."

She smiles against my mouth and slips her hand around me again. "Okay, you can come, Mason. *Now*."

Her mouth slams down on mine as she works my cock relentlessly, swallowing my moans until I can't hold back anymore.

I come with her name on my lips, my vision turning white as pleasure crashes over me. She strokes me through it, milking every drop from my cock until I'm boneless and gasping as she murmurs soft praise against my ear.

When she releases the restraints, my arms fall to my sides like they're made of Jell-o. She disappears briefly, returning with a warm washcloth to clean me up.

"Where did you—you're too young to—never mind, I

don't care. You're...fucking amazing." I struggle to find words as she settles beside me on the bed.

A satisfied smile tugs at her lips.

I turn to face her, wanting desperately to return the favor. Her hand on my chest stops me.

"Rest," she says softly. "We've got all night."

I draw her close, burying my nose in her hair, breathing in the scent that's suddenly become my favorite drug. As sleep pulls at me, one thought bursts through the post-orgasmic haze.

I am completely and utterly hers.

Whether she knows it yet or not.

CHAPTER 6
REMI

I wake to the velvet drag of Mason's tongue and morning stubble trailing down my stomach.

He pins my hips to the mattress, his lips grazing the sensitive skin of my inner thighs as he works his way inside. In the dim predawn light, the sight of him between my legs makes me shudder.

"My turn," he murmurs, his voice still rough with sleep. "I need to taste you."

Last night comes flooding back—me taking control, pushing him to the edge over and over, watching him fall apart under my hands. And him giving himself to me completely, surrendering in a way I never expected from a man like him.

Now, instead of diving right in, he takes his time, pressing soft kisses along the crease of my hips and thighs, maddeningly close to my pussy, deliberately avoiding where I need him most. His warm breath teases my wet center, making me squirm with anticipation.

"Someone's very eager," he chuckles, nipping at my skin.

"Mason…" I whine.

"Patience," he counters, his smile positively wicked. "You made me wait last night, remember? Fair's fair."

His lips and tongue tease over me, his intense blue eyes watching my reactions. Every time I arch toward his mouth, he pulls back slightly, denying me what I want.

"Bastard," I hiss, my fingers tightening in his hair.

"Just enjoying the view," he murmurs, his breath hot against my sensitive flesh. "You're so fucking beautiful like this, Remi, all wet and wanting."

When he finally presses his mouth fully against me, the relief is so intense I nearly jerk off the bed. His tongue is masterful—broad, flat strokes alternating with gentle precision that has me seeing stars. The contrast of his soft tongue and rough stubble creates a sensation that's addicting.

"Been dreaming about this," he groans, the vibration making me gasp. "The way you'd taste, the sounds you'd make. But god, it's even better than I imagined."

My hips rock, but his strong hands hold me firmly in place, his forearms creating a delicious weight pressing across my thighs.

"Stay still," he commands, pupils dilated. "Let me worship you properly."

Every swipe of his tongue feels like he's mapping me, learning what makes me tremble and moan. He finds a rhythm that has me clutching the sheets, my back bowing as tension winds tighter and tighter in my core.

Just as I'm about to topple over the edge, he slows down, pulling back to snake his tongue around my pubic bone and inner thighs.

"Don't you dare stop, asshole," I warn, my voice a breathless rasp.

He laughs darkly. "Oh, I'm not stopping. Just making it last."

When his mouth returns to me, he focuses entirely on working my clit, and the intensity doubles. He alternates between teasing licks and gentle suction, then firm circular motions that have me gasping his name.

Soon, I'm moaning *loudly*, wondering when our neighbors will get sick of the noise and pound on the wall, yelling at us to shut up.

Mason seems to love it. "That's it, baby," he encourages, looking up at me as he drives me crazy. "I want to hear you come for me."

The orgasm builds like a gathering storm, the tension increasing until finally it breaks.

"Fuck!!!" My body convulses, pleasure tearing through me. My thighs clamp down around his head, but he doesn't stop. He draws out my pleasure until I'm shaking, oversensitive, pushing weakly at his shoulders.

Before I can catch my breath, he's moving up my body, his cock hot, hard and heavy against my thigh.

He pauses at my breasts. "Dammit, your tits are perfect." He takes a peak into his mouth, sucking and teasing with his tongue and teeth until I'm squirming beneath him again, the aftershocks of pleasure like so many lightning bolts.

"Condom," I manage to gasp.

He reaches for his wallet on the nightstand, retrieving a foil packet. I take it from him, rolling it onto his impressive length as he watches me with hooded eyes.

"You sure?" he asks, a gentleman even now when he's trembling with need.

My answer is to hook my leg around his waist and pull him toward me. He sinks into my pussy with one powerful thrust, both of us groaning at the sensation.

"Jesus Christ, Remi," he breathes, stilling for a moment to let me adjust to his size. "You feel spectacular."

He fills me completely, stretching me with his thick steel rod. When he starts to move, it's with long, deep strokes that have me clawing at his back.

"More," I demand, digging my heels into his ass.

His rhythm falters for a moment before he grabs my wrists, pinning them over my head as he drives into me with renewed force. The change in angle has him hitting exactly where I need him, and I feel myself building toward another release, my entire body shaking.

"Look at me," he growls. "Fuck, Remi. You're so goddamn beautiful."

Something in his gaze undoes me, whether it's the raw vulnerability, the naked desire, or the way he sees me and only me. It sends me careening over the edge again, my pussy clenching around him as I detonate, moaning his name.

"Fuck!" he groans, following me over the edge moments later, his hips erratic as they buck and jerk. He finally shudders above me before collapsing onto my chest, both of us panting and drenched in sweat.

We lie tangled together for a long moment, his weight comforting rather than crushing. He presses a kiss onto my shoulder, then rolls off me, getting rid of the condom before pulling me into his side.

"I'm really liking this," he says softly, tracing patterns on my bare thigh.

The tender moment, the intimacy, the way we fit together so perfectly—it scares the hell out of me. Because beneath the physical pleasure lurks a dangerous truth: I'm falling for this man.

I slide out of bed, suddenly needing some space. "We should get ready. Day two of the show starts in an hour."

His face falls slightly, but he recovers quickly. "Yeah. Of course."

In the shower, I let the scalding water beat down on my shoulders, trying to wash away the confusion clouding my mind. In my head, this was supposed to be just sex...hot, mind-blowing sex with a guy I've been lusting after despite my better judgment. Not...whatever this tightness is in my chest whenever he looks at me with those puppy dog eyes.

By the time we arrive at the bike show, I'm professional, focused, keeping a careful space between us as we talk to potential clients.

Mason keeps shooting me confused glances, his brow furrowing beneath his backward baseball cap, hurt flickering across his face when I deftly evade his casual touches. But what choice do I have? He's fielded *three fucking calls* from that TV producer already this morning.

Just before lunch, I overhear him on the phone again, standing a little way off by the coffee station.

"I appreciate the offer, Mark, but I need some time to think about it," he says, running a hand through his hair. "Yes, I understand it's a great opportunity... No, I'm not just playing hard to get."

God damn it. I knew it. The bright lights are already calling him back, and I'm going to be just another notch in his tool belt —a temporary distraction while he plots his triumphant return to fame.

When he returns to our booth, I'm frostier than ever.

"Everything okay?" he asks, concern etching his stupidly handsome features.

"Just peachy," I snap, turning to greet an approaching customer with a practiced smile.

The day drags on endlessly. By evening, the tension between us has become suffocating. We barely speak as we pack up the booth for the night.

Back at the hotel, I head straight for the shower, needing

the barrier of steam and tile between us. When I emerge, Mason is sitting on the edge of the bed, his expression serious.

"Are we going to talk about what happened?" he asks.

"Nothing happened," I lie, busying myself with packing up my clothes. "We had sex. It was fun. The end."

He stands, frustration evident in the set of his shoulders. "Bullshit. You've been avoiding me all day."

"We're here to work. Not play house."

"Is this about the phone calls? Because if it is—"

"It's about *reality*, Mason," I spit, anger flaring hot and sudden. "You know all about reality, don't you? You're obviously weighing your options for getting back on TV. And why wouldn't you? It's what you wanted before."

Pain crosses his face like a shadow. "I'm not that person anymore, Remi. I thought I'd proved that to you."

"With what? A few orgasms? Some pretty words?" I laugh, the sound brittle even to me. "Actions speak louder than words. Come on, your finger's still hovering over that producer's number."

"I haven't said yes," he says through gritted teeth.

"You haven't said no, either," I counter. "I refuse to be collateral damage in your comeback story, Mason."

He steps back like I've slapped him. "I can't believe you think I'm using you."

The hurt in his voice makes me falter, guilt tugging at my resolve. But I can't back down now—not when my heart feels it might shatter if I let him any closer.

"I… I think you don't know what you want," I finally say quietly. "And I'm not going to wait around while you figure it out."

He stares at me for a long moment.

"You're scared," he says at last, his voice soft. "Not of me leaving, but of what happens if I stay."

His perceptiveness cuts way too close to the bone. Because I *am* terrified. Of falling for him completely. Of building something real, only to see it crumble.

"You should get some sleep," I mutter, turning away to hide the tears threatening to spill. "We've got another long day tomorrow."

I slip under the covers, my back to him, creating a wall of tension between us. The bed dips as he climbs in on his side, maintaining the distance I've enforced.

In the darkness, I listen to his breathing slowly even out, wondering how something that felt so right this morning could hurt so much now.

CHAPTER 7
MASON

I haven't slept. Not really. How could I, with Remi's words still echoing in my mind?

You don't know what you want. I'm not going to wait around while you figure it out.

She's already gone when I wake up in the morning—for breakfast, I assume.

I rub my eyes, feeling every one of my thirty-nine years in the stiffness of my shoulders. I thought she and I were moving forward. Those moments in bed, her surrender, the vulnerability in her eyes, they'd felt like a beginning.

I guess I'd forgotten how fear can nibble at your courage. How it can make you push away the very thing you're afraid to lose.

My phone buzzes. Mark's name flashes on the screen for the umpteenth time since yesterday. I stare at it, remembering Remi's accusation.

Your finger's still hovering over that producer's number.

She's right. I've been waffling, thinking maybe I *could* have both—the life I'm building in Deepwood, plus the validation of being wanted again by the industry that previously chewed me up and spit me out.

I tap "accept," bringing the phone to my ear.

"Mason! About time," Mark crows. "Look, we need an answer today. The network's chomping at the bit. Whaddya say?"

I close my eyes, picturing the bright lights, the cameras, the hollow adoration. Then I see Remi's face...fierce, genuine, challenging me to be a better man than I ever have.

"It's a no, Mark," I say, my voice steady. "I'm exactly where I need to be."

"What? Are you fucking *kidding* me?" His disbelief squawks through the line. "You're crazy, Mason. You'll never get another chance like this."

"I know." I find myself smiling. "And that's okay."

I hang up before he can launch into another pitch, then with great satisfaction block his number. The relief is immediate, like I've set down a weight I've been carrying for too long.

But turning down the show isn't going to be enough for Remi. She demands proof, not promises.

A crazy plan that's been percolating for days suddenly crystallizes. I grab my phone again and call the one person who might be able to help me pull it off.

"Lily? It's Mason. I need a huge favor."

The last day of the bike expo passes in a blur, and we somehow make it back to Deepwood with our professional masks firmly in place. The drive home was excruciating... Remi white-knuckling the steering wheel and blasting angry death metal the entire way, me staring out the window like a zombie, both of us drowning in unsaid words.

The following week, I'm the first one in the shop and the last one out every day. Dash notices, of course—nothing gets past him—but he doesn't object when I ask to use the back bay after hours.

Lily helps with designs, staying late a couple of nights when I need an extra set of hands or her artistic eye. She insisted, despite not feeling well.

Remi watches me every so often, and I can tell she's suspicious of my late nights and the way I've been hiding away in the far corner of the garage. She catches me hunched over sketches during lunch breaks, quickly tucking them away when she approaches. I've caught her lingering near my workstation when she thinks I'm not looking, too.

By the seventh day, it's ready.

"Hey, Remi," I say as everyone's packing up for the night. "Can you stick around for a bit?"

She glances up from where she's wiping grease off her hands, wariness in her eyes. "Why?"

"Just want to show you something."

She hesitates. "Fine," she finally says, tossing the rag into a wash bin. "But I'm not staying long."

I wait while Zane, Kyle, and Dax file out, their knowing glances making my ears burn. Dash is the last to leave, winking as he walks out.

Finally, Remi and I are alone. "What's going on?" she asks apprehensively. "You've been avoiding me. Sneaking in early. Staying late. Kyle says I broke you."

I chuckle. "You haven't exactly said more than a few words to me either, and only when it's necessary for work." I gesture toward the back bay where a heavy black tarp covers my surprise. "Just—come with me. Please?"

She sighs but follows as I lead her further into the garage.

My heart hammers against my ribs as I turn to her. "I

turned Mark down," I say without preamble. "Told him I'm not coming back to TV. Ever."

Her eyes widen slightly, but she still looks defensive. "Well... Good for you."

"I actually did it before we left Boulder," I continue. "But I knew that wouldn't be enough for you. So I've been working on something."

I move to the tarp, my fingers curling around the edge. "This is for you, Remi. To show you exactly what I want."

With a deep breath, I pull the tarp off.

The motorcycle gleams under the shop lights, a custom bobber built from the ground up. The frame is sleek and aggressive, painted black with metallic neon green accents that mimic the streaks in her hair. The gas tank bears a hand-painted raven in flight, its wings stretching toward the handle-bars. The black leather seat is butter-soft, stitched with intricate patterns that mirror Remi's favorite tattoos.

It's unlike anything I've ever built—not for show or for television, not for anyone's approval but hers. Every curve, every detail speaks to who she is: fierce, independent, uncompromising.

Remi's lips part in shock, her arms falling to her sides as she steps closer.

"How did you..." She circles the bike in disbelief, trailing her fingers over the custom exhaust pipes and handcrafted foot pegs.

"I worked hard and fast." I swallow. "And Lily helped with the raven design. I wanted it to be perfect for you."

She runs her hand along the tank, her fingers shaking slightly. "You built this for me?"

"Everything about it *is* you, Remi. The way it doesn't give a shit about convention. How it's built for both power and beauty." I step closer, my voice dropping. "It's as fearless as you are."

She looks up at me, her tough exterior cracking just enough to let me see the vulnerability beneath. "Why?"

"Because I'm all in, Remi. Not just with you, but this life—the shop, Deepwood Mountain, all of it." I rake a hand through my hair. "Fame was like a drug. It gave me everything and left me with nothing. But you... You gave me something to prove. A reason to be better."

Her fingers trace the raven's wing. "That's, um, a lot of pressure to put on someone."

"Please don't think of it that way." I gesture to the bike. "This isn't a bribe or a grand gesture to sweep you off your feet. It's just tangible proof that *I see you*, and I'm not going anywhere."

Something shifts in her eyes. "You really turned him down?"

"Blocked his number and everything," I confirm. "And I'd do it again in a heartbeat. Honestly? It felt great."

A small smile tugs at her lips.

I step into her space, slowly enough that she could move away if she wanted to.

But she doesn't.

Halle—fuckin—lujah.

"All I'm asking is if you'll give us a real shot." My fingers find hers tentatively. "I know I'm older. I know I've fucked up. But I also know that what's between us is worth fighting for."

"I dunno… You're still a reality TV has-been," she says, but there's a wicked sparkle in her eye.

"And you're still the most talented mechanic I know, who scares the shit out of me," I counter. "In the sexiest possible way, of course."

She laughs, the sound washing over me like morning sunlight. "God, we're a mess."

"The best kind," I agree, pulling her closer.

Her hand slides up my chest to rest on my thundering heart. "If you ever—"

"Please," I beg. "Trust that I mean this, Remi. Every word."

She studies me for a long moment, then rises on her tiptoes to press her lips to mine. This kiss is different from our others —not desperate, or angry, or lustful. Something deeper.

Maybe it's love.

"So," she murmurs against my lips. "When do I get to ride it?"

I grin, unable to resist. "My cock? Right now, if you want. The shop's empty—"

Her eyes darken with heat. "I meant the motorcycle, meathead."

"Hey, why not both?" I reply, backing her against the bike and capturing her mouth in a hungry kiss.

Fuck, I've missed this...

She reaches for my belt buckle. My hands slide down her sides, tugging at her work pants. She shimmies them down along with her little black panties before sitting sideways on the bike, the custom leather seat cradling her sweet ass.

I drop to my knees before her, nudging her thighs apart. "I think your new bike needs christening," I murmur, looking up at her with lust in my eyes. "And to do that I'm going to eat your beautiful pussy right here, right now."

She tangles her fingers in my hair, her lips parted, eyelids hooded with want. "Such a romantic."

We have a lot to figure out: her apartment versus my parents' place (who am I kidding? Definitely her apartment), not to mention working together every day. But right now, all that matters is the scrape of her nails against my scalp and the sound of her delicious moans. And mostly, the soft, whispered "I love you" as she throws her head back in ecstasy.

It's not at all the life I pictured for myself years ago, standing in front of cameras with fame at my fingertips.

It's much, much better.

The next morning, I'm buffing away the marks we left on the bike's chrome when there's a commotion in the office and the door bursts open.

"Holy *shit!*" Kyle's voice echoes off the rafters. "Is that the St. Claire Special?"

Dash follows behind him. His eyebrows shoot up when his gaze lands on the bike. "You built this, Mason?"

Remi saunters over from the workbench, coffee in hand. Her smug smile could power the Deepwood electrical grid. "Yep. All by his lonesome, too. Even got the carburetor ratios right."

Kyle gawks, eyes traveling between the two of us, then widening. "Excuse me? Since when do you two—"

Dax comes up and smacks the back of Kyle's head. "Took you long enough, idiot."

The rest of the crew rolls in, Zane grunting his approval, Lily tearfully hugging us both.

"But...*fuck!*" Kyle groans. "I made a bet with Ellie that if you two got together I'd have to detail the food truck. *Naked!*"

"Pics or it didn't happen," Remi says, then freezes. "On second thought—never mind. I don't want to be scarred for life."

Everyone but Kyle laughs, who's still kicking the ground with his boot.

Dash pulls me aside, his grip firm on my shoulder. "Nice work, Mason. On the bike…and with Remi. Proud of you."

His words make my chest puff out. Well, shit. Maybe *this* was the validation I really wanted all along.

Before I can respond, I see Remi hop onto her new bike, revving the engine, the roar drowning out the hubbub around us.

"Out of the way!" she yells. "We're test driving!"

I grab a helmet and swing on behind her, my arms wrapping around her waist as she guns it onto the open road. Wind whips our laughter into the Montana sky, the world blurring into streaks of green and asphalt.

She turns her head and flips up her visor. "Where to, old man?"

I tighten my hold on her, grinning. "Wherever you are, baby. Wherever you are."

EPILOGUE - REMI

SIX MONTHS LATER

The bed's empty when I wake up. I know Mason's probably in the bathroom, as per his usual morning routine.

The scent of coffee drifts in from the kitchen thanks to the automatic machine I programmed last night—one of the few modern conveniences I insisted on when Mason moved into my apartment six months ago. His parents were probably relieved. I mean, having your middle-aged son bring home his tattooed, green-haired girlfriend to meet the family was awkward enough. But sleepovers in their house with its paper-thin walls? Yeah, not fun for anyone.

I slide carefully from the sheets, pulling on Mason's discarded T-shirt from yesterday. It hangs to mid-thigh and smells like his spicy deodorant and natural musk. I pad across the hardwood, heading toward caffeine salvation.

To my surprise, Mason's already there, wearing nothing but low-slung boxers, flipping pancakes with the practiced ease of someone who's been cooking Sunday brunch for months. He's humming some Bon Jovi song with *way* too much gusto.

"Morning, sleepyhead," he says without turning, somehow

sensing my presence like always. "Thought you'd sleep till noon after last night."

Heat floods my cheeks at the memory—Mason on his knees, me straddling his face, nearly ripping the headboard in half. He's already promised to bolt the damn thing to the wall today.

"You wore me out," I admit, sliding my arms around his waist, pressing my cheek against the warm expanse of his back. "But the smell of coffee woke me up."

"Thought it might," he chuckles, the sound vibrating through his body into mine. "And the blueberry pancakes are almost done."

"God, I love you," I murmur, the words still new on my tongue, the taste simultaneously sweet and terrifying.

Mason turns, spatula in hand, to press a kiss to my forehead. "Love you too, sexy."

I smile as I grab a mug from the cabinet. The kitchen's become our shared domain—half my organized chaos, half his meticulous order. Somehow, it works.

Like us.

I settle in at the breakfast bar, the light catching the silver streaks in his temples as he works. I've long stopped teasing him about it. Truth is, I love our age difference. His extra life experience balances my impulsiveness, just as my energy keeps him from settling into old patterns. He's lived long enough to know what matters, but not so much that he's forgotten how to have fun.

Like when he begs me to tie him to the bed. *Rowr.*

"What's the plan for today?" he asks, startling me out of my daydreams and sliding a perfect stack of pancakes in front of me.

"Absolutely nothing," I answer, drenching them in syrup. "Unless Lily texts that she's going into labor early." Turns out she wasn't feeling well a few months ago because she was preggers!

"Hey, there's still two more months," Mason reminds me, sitting beside me with his own plate. "Poor Zane. Did you see him baby-proofing the parts closet yesterday?"

I think back to when Lily announced her pregnancy by tossing a positive test onto the shop counter like a spark plug order. Zane had gone sheet-white and nearly toppled a Harley. Now, he's building a sidecar crib. Awesome.

I snort. "Kyle was worse when he and Ellie got the call from the adoption agency about their baby girl from Colombia. I've only seen him cry once in my life, and that was when he slammed his finger in his toolbox. But on the phone, he was sobbing." I tear up just thinking about it. *Stupid Kyle.*

"How the mighty have fallen," Mason chuckles. "All of us, taken down by love."

"Eww. Gross," I say, but can't hide my smile.

After breakfast, we migrate to the couch—me with my latest horror novel, Mason with the football game on TV. At some point my feet end up in his lap, his strong fingers kneading my soles absent-mindedly. Pure contentment swims through my veins, thick and sweet as honey.

I glance at him over my book, studying his profile. The pride he takes in his work now has nothing to do with cameras or recognition, and everything to do with the craft itself, the joy of creating something beautiful and functional with his hands.

Everyone notices. Just last week, Dash offered all of us partnership in the shop, if we wanted it.

Of course, we all accepted. Duhh.

Then we'd thrown an impromptu celebration, Kyle and Ellie bringing Mexican food, Dax and Kendra supplying stupid expensive champagne, and Lily and Zane sharing their latest ultrasound photos. Just our motley chosen family, forged in chrome and grease.

"Hey," Mason says, noticing my blank stare. "Book not violent enough?"

I shake myself. "Just thinking."

"Dangerous pastime," he teases, switching the TV off with the remote and turning toward me. He seems suddenly nervous, fingers tapping my ankle. "Actually, I've been thinking too."

"About?"

"About us." He reaches behind the couch cushion and produces a small wooden box. "About how you've completely turned my world upside down."

My heart stutters. "Mason…"

"Just listen, okay? Please?" He takes a deep breath. "I know the idea of marriage makes you twitchy. And I know you value your independence more than anything—it's one of the million reasons I fell in love with you."

He opens the box, revealing a custom-crafted ring. The band is polished steel with intricate tooling that resembles motorcycle gears, inlaid with tiny onyxes and diamonds.

It's gorgeous.

"This doesn't have to change anything about who you are or how we live," he barrels on, his strong voice rough with emotion. "It's just…a promise. That I'll always be your biggest fan, your fiercest supporter, and the guy who will hold your tools when you ask me to."

Tears prick my eyes.

"I had Dax help me forge it from parts of that first bike we worked on together," he grins. "That Ducati that almost killed us both with its deadline."

A strangled laugh escapes me. "That fucking bike."

"Yeah." His smile is unsteady. "So…Remi St. Claire, terror

of the motorcycle world, woman who brings me to my knees in all the best ways...will you marry me?"

Six months ago, I would have run screaming from this moment.

But now?

"Yes," I whisper, then clear my throat and say it a little louder. "Yes, I'll marry you...you sentimental meathead."

His face splits into a grin that takes years off his age as he slides the ring onto my finger. It's a perfect fit. Of course it is.

"One condition," I say as he pulls me into his lap.

"Anything."

"I'm keeping my last name. And we're having the ceremony at the garage, and I'm wearing black."

Mason laughs, wrapping his arms around me. "That's three conditions, babe. But it's all good. I wouldn't have it any other way."

His mouth meets mine, tenderly at first, then with a hunger that never seems to diminish no matter how many times we come together. I press closer, feeling the hard planes of his chest against mine, his heart racing.

"We should celebrate," I murmur into his lips, already tugging at his boxers.

"All damn day," he agrees, hands sliding under my shirt.

Now that we've come to the end of the McCafferty Mechanics series...what's next?

Lumberjacks of Timber Run

Visit the wild forests of Timber Run, a former logging frontier of Deepwood Mountain, Montana, where a group of rugged lumberjacks with calloused hands and powerful physiques have built more than just a historic lumberjack reenactment camp.

These mountain men know their way around an axe and sizable wood, but when it comes to love? They're about to be cut down to size.

Each burly bachelor thought they had their path mapped out, until the right woman came along to show them that the most beautiful things grow in untamed places.

Get swept off your feet by the irresistible, brawny men of Timber Run, and surrender to the kind of passion only found in their unexpectedly tender hearts.

Check out the Lumberjacks of Timber Run series page: https://www.lexihayes.com/series/lumberjacks-of-timber-run

You can sign up for my newsletter and get a FREE book via my website:
www.lexihayes.com
It's the best way to hear about new and upcoming releases, plus get access to subscriber exclusives and bonus content.

And as always, if you liked this book, please post a review on any of your preferred platforms. Reviews are the lifeblood of independent authors like me, and I welcome your opinions and feedback.

Thanks for reading!

ABOUT THE AUTHOR

Lexi writes short, steamy, over-the-top romance with a heaping dose of humor. She's a long-time superhero lover, book sniffer, and Mr. Darcy fanatic. Raised in the same SoCal city as Will Ferrell, she now resides in sweltering Las Vegas with her husband and the ghosts of two spoiled cats. She dreams of lush green foliage, ocean waves, and Henry Cavill. Or Alan Ritchson. It's a toss-up really. ;)

Join Lexi's mailing list for new and upcoming releases (and FREE book!) here: www.lexihayes.com

f facebook.com/lexihayesauthor
O instagram.com/lexihayesauthor

www.ingramcontent.com/pod-product-compliance
Lightning Source LLC
Chambersburg PA
CBHW020119180626
46812CB00006B/2660